William Clark Russell

The Golden Hope

Vol. 3

William Clark Russell

The Golden Hope
Vol. 3

ISBN/EAN: 9783337347017

Printed in Europe, USA, Canada, Australia, Japan

Cover: Foto ©Andreas Hilbeck / pixelio.de

More available books at **www.hansebooks.com**

A ROMANCE OF THE DEEP

.

BY

W. CLARK RUSSELL

AUTHOR OF

"A SEA QUEEN," "THE WRECK OF THE GROSVENOR," "A SAILOR'S SWEETHEART,"
ETC., ETC.

"I had a dream which was not all a dream"

IN THREE VOLUMES

VOL. III

LONDON

HURST AND BLACKETT, LIMITED
13, GREAT MARLBOROUGH STREET
1887

PRINTED BY

TILLOTSON AND SON, MAWDSLEY STREET

BOLTON.

CONTENTS

OF

THE THIRD VOLUME.

CHAPTER.	PAGE.
I.—THE TANGLED HAIR	I
II.—THE DREAMER	32
III.—A STEAMER IS SIGHTED . . .	48
IV.—THE SCHOONER IS SPOKEN .	71
V.—A NEW PASSENGER . . .	91
VI.—THE BABY IS FED	115
VII.—THE BLINDNESS OF THE MIND . . .	133
VIII.—STONE ADVISES	151
IX.—OVERBOARD	171
X.—THE BURIAL OF THE BABY	189
XI.—THE NEW DAWN	228
XII.—HOME	262

THE GOLDEN HOPE.

CHAPTER I.

THE TANGLED HAIR.

In purchasing an outfit of apparel, in the conviction that he would find Agatha, Fortescue had forgotten to include either bonnets or hats! The oversight seems strange, yet it was not so strange as the perception he had shown in his other purchases. What was to be done? He reflected a minute and then recollected that he had a sealskin cap. He fetched it and placed it on Agatha's head. It fitted her well; the rich stuff, by contrast, put a ruddier fire into the gold colour of her hair, and the beauty of her face seemed perfected by it. There was a strip of looking-glass upon the bulkhead near her cabin, and Fortescue, bent on striving to penetrate her memory by any sort of agent that offered, asked her, while he pointed to the glass, to tell him if she liked the cap. She looked and smiled, blushing, and adjusted it to her taste.

" It is very pretty," she said, " but my hair makes me appear dreadfully wild."

" Do you know the person you are looking at ?" he asked.

" I am looking at myself?" she replied, in an interrogative manner, as though prepared to be told she was mistaken.

" And do you know who you are ?"

" You have told me : I am Agatha Fox."

" And I ?"

" You are Mr. Fortescue."

" The Reverend Malcolm Fortescue, curate of St. James's, Wyloe ; an intimate friend of the vicar, the Reverend Alfred Clayton, and of your step-father, Dr. Joseph Clayton. My darling, look in the glass as I pronounce these names——"

She interrupted him. " Why do you call me your darling ?"

"We were to have been married. We
are still betrothed. If God suffers us to
reach England you will be my wife."

She stared at him. It was unquestion-
able that she understood the meaning of
his words *as* words; but as they were not
referable to any matter determinable by her
consciousness, their significance as a speech
was unintelligible to her. She dropped her
eyes with a sigh, and began to play with
her hair.

"It'll seem disheartening work, sir," said
Archer, standing up against the bunk in
the bulkhead, waiting for Fortescue and
Agatha to go on deck before "turning in,"
"but don't give up. It's trying as'll do it."

"There's no fear of my giving up," said
the clergyman, quietly. "If I were of a
giving up nature I should not be here."

"No, sir, nor the lady, nor me; God
bless you!"

"There is one question I have forgotten
to ask you. Have you any idea in which
of the boats Miss Fox's step-father went?"

"You mean Dr. Clayton? No, sir, I
cannot tell. There was tremendous con-

, *f̵.*

fusion at the last. All the ladies, I believe, were to have gone in the captain's boat, the long-boat, I think. Perhaps Dr. Clayton was in her, as he would expect Miss Fox to be there. How she got into my boat I don't know. I found her there, and my-self in charge. I understand from a man forrards that only one of the boats had been accounted for at the time of your starting."

"Only one—the boat that was in charge of the third mate."

"Ha! it was a bad job—a bad job!" exclaimed Archer.

"I presume you never called the lady by her name. She did not seem to know it until I told her."

"I don't suppose I did, sir. I can't recollect. This side her memory I mayn't. I always called her Miss. I'd speak of her to the others as Miss Fox, but to her face as Miss."

Fortescue took Agatha's hand and con-ducted her on deck. It was about three o'clock; the sun stood in glory over the top-gallant yard-arm; wool-white clouds trailed in steam-like wreaths along the hard blue that paled and deepened under the brassy glare, as if the trade-wind blew in azure folds, rising and falling like the swell of the sea; all around was staring ocean running away in burnished backs of golden splendour north-west and coming up from the south-east, blue, sweet, foam-edged, full of fountain-like murmurings, and each near sea as it arched, flung with its burden of spray a touch of salt coolness into the wind. The schooner was showing every inch of canvas that would draw; her tall tapering masts swept their radiant cloths under the blue sky to a regular swinging leaning that timed the cadence of the little seas as a conductor's baton would a solemn music. The wake flashed fair north-east, and at the extremity of it trembled a blotch of greenish film—the island.

With her hair blowing about her, her eyes on fire with the sparkling daylight, her lips parted, her bosom heaving fast, Agatha stood at the head of the companion-steps, with her hand in Fortescue's as though entranced. She glanced swiftly from one

object to another, from the shining decks to
the canvas, from the windward running
ridges to the glory on the leeward sea, and
so on to right round the horizon, and then
exclaimed softly, " How beautiful ! You said
we are going home ?"

" Yes, I said I had come to take you
home. You remember that ?"

She nodded, looking about her with eager,
fascinated eyes. He led her to the taffrail.
Old Breeches was at the tiller, and she gave
him a nod and a smile, to which he responded with a drag at a coil of hair upon his
forehead. This recognition was one of the
most pronounced illustrations of the phe-
nomenal condition of her mind that had yet
occurred. It was perfectly certain the faculty
of memory could not be dead in her, for she
recollected the old seaman the moment she
saw him. Why, then, should its powers be
limited to this side of the curtain that had
fallen? Why, behind the veil, should it be
blind and deaf and mute?

" Do you see that little spot—that little
shadow yonder ?" the curate exclaimed, pointing.

" Plainly."

" It is the island we are carrying you away from, where you have been solitary, and hopeless, and unheeded, save by the eye of Almighty God, for nine months, Agatha. For nine months, my precious one. Can you realise that time?" He looked at her clasping her hair with her right hand to prevent it from blowing across her face, at her delicately-carven, most beautiful profile, cameo-like against the blue, at the searching grey eyes softened into tenderness inexpressible by the shadowing of the lashes, at her figure full of the free and floating grace of some wild bird that alights on a swaying branch and poises itself a moment ere folding its wings. Great God! with what passion did his heart yearn towards her then, for the encounter of her eyes, and for the light of her knowledge of him in them! But instead of answering him she whispered to herself, and then breaking from whatever fancies were in her, she released her hand and ran to the compass, and like a child stood looking into it with a smiling face. Thence, all about the deck, her lover following her and the men furtively watching her. If ever there was music in movement it was in the floating, buoyant measures of her gait. Archer came very near to the truth when he described it as a waltzing motion. She went right into the bows, and catching sight of the golden figure-head, leaned over the rail with a backward glance at Fortescue to join her; and as he looked with her, firmly grasping her hand and listening to her as she pointed to the reflection of the gilded angel in every lucent blue hollow ere the sliding stem crushed a boiling whiteness over it, and as she turned with delighted exclamations to survey the heights of canvas impelling the sharp bows shearing through the billows, he wondered if this new birth of hers, this emergence of fresh intellectual life out of the blankness that had been wrought in her by misery and fiendish insult, was not an illustration of the birth of the soul through the dissolution of the body, was not identical with the new existence of the spirit after death.

It might have been the spirit of freedom that had come to her as a gift from the island in replacement of the priceless faculty that was suspended or partially destroyed, which caused her to detain Fortescue for a long while in the bows, whilst with sparkling eyes and swiftly-moving bosom, and a sympathetic movement of her admirable figure, she watched the graceful dance of the surge, the winged leap of the schooner, the burst of many-coloured lustre in the heart of the smoking spray as the fierce slide of the cut-water hurled the snow to the cathead and sent it seething to the sun. At last he induced her to walk aft with him, and the little awning being spread, he placed a chair for her under it.

Old Stone stumped the deck to windward, feigning to see nothing but the weather and the schooner; Breeches at the tiller steered doggedly, leisurely gnawing upon a piece of tobacco in his cheek, so that by the motion of his jaws he appeared to be grumbling mutinously to himself; a couple of men stitched upon a sail in the waist; another was in the forerigging busy with a ratline or two; the cook went in and out of the caboose and talked to the boy Johnny, who was washing dishes in a bucket to leeward;

the smudge of island had vanished, the sea-
line ran round clear and clean as glass, and
the warm wind poured its steady strain into
the leaning hollows of the canvas.   For a
moment or so a profound sense of unreality
oppressed Fortescue.   He looked at Agatha
seated beside him, he looked round the
mighty sea, at the place where the island
had vanished, that island which had engrossed his thoughts, apprehensions, hopes,
for months and months, which had come and
now was gone, he looked at the schooner
sailing along with the same infinite ocean-
distance under her jibbooms that had been
there ever since the English coast had been
lost sight of, at the men quietly going on
with their work with the astonishing experience of the day already fitting easily
upon their moods, after the true fashion of
sailors, in whom amazement is but a weakly
emotion, thanks to the endless wonders the
mariner encounters ; and then, thinking of
his dream, how it had been realised, how
compassionately true had been the pointing
of the visionary Finger, how now there sat
beside him, within reach of hand and lip, the

girl he adored, whom he had sometimes imagined lost to him for ever, whom he had parted with in sickness and had found in physical health, and beautiful with a beauty that was like a spirit in her—a sort of numbness seized his brain, nothing seemed conceivable but the sense of the unreality that possessed him.

But the strange, distracting, dangerous sensation passed, yet not until it had bathed his brow with sweat and ran tremor after tremor, as of ague, through his body.

"Agatha," he exclaimed, gently, after giving himself a little time, "do you never feel as if there is something missing, something behind all that has happened upon the island, all you remember that has happened?"

"What is missing?" she asked.

"Cannot you conceive that you lived before you were wrecked upon the island, and that many more things must have happened then than since?"

"I cannot remember," she answered. "I have no memory, I know that. It hurts me when I think. A pain comes here," touching her forehead, "a pain like a weight."

" Do you remember the Verulam ?"

" No."

" Do you remember the long, long days you spent in the open boat?"

" No."

" Have you no recollection of the boat being tossed over in the surf, and you and Archer struggling to the land?"

She shook her head whilst she shaded her eyes with her hand and hung her face.

" Do you remember Archer and Williams building the little house of trees and leaves I found you in ?"

She looked up quickly and answered, " Yes." He saw that she was crying ; her tears struck him to the soul.

" My own, my darling !" he murmured, smoothing her hand with touching gestures of endearment. " It will come, it will come ! The mercy I implore will be vouchsafed. I must have patience. It is my heart-sickness for one look of recognition from you that makes me cruel in my anxiety——" He ceased, observing her to smile through her tears, yet with a smile that gave him to see if he were speaking to a child three years old he could not be less understood.

Yet one point he noticed through the questions he had put to her: that any effort that forced her to think back into the darkness of the past produced actual pain—a sense of weight and aching over the brows. He felt it was an early hint to him he must bear in mind, otherwise how was he to guess what mischief might be wrought to her brain by compelling such intellectual powers as were left to worry and work upon the faculty that had been weakened, numbed, paralysed —call its condition what you will. So for half-an-hour he sat lightly talking to her, just quietly observing in her such differing manners as she exhibited whilst she listened, or answered, or addressed him.

Taking up a tress of her hair, he said, "Agatha, you used to wear this wreathed upon your head like a crown. Can all these tangles be brushed out of it? I will try, if you will let me."

"I tried myself; it will be hard to smooth it. You can try, but you will have to be patient. See how full of knots it is." She

thrust her fingers through it to let him
observe she could not comb them down an
inch.   The heave of the schooner would
bring the brightness on the sea flowing off
the waters in a gush under the awning, and
at such times her hair, fluffy with innumerable single hairs curling out of the dense
mass, flashed like a surface of spangles and
shed a light around her head that was as a
frame for her sun-touched beauty.

Stone, pacing to windward, took a squint
at her now and again out of the corners of
his eyes.   When they went below the old
fellow said to Breeches, " Bill, did you ever
see hair like that afore?"

" Well, I dunno as ever I did."

" Did ye ever see a finer figure afore?"

" Well, I'll not say 'yes' to that, neither!
But it's a sorter fineness more relishable in
daylight than when the moon's a-shining.   I
don't mind owning to it, if I'd ha' bin sent to
that there island, and she'd ha' come leaping
along to me with that dancing walk of hers,
smite me if I don't think I'd 'a shoved off and
lay-tew for consideration.   Any man can see
what it's all about now; but to come upon the

likes of her, fresh—with such hair blowin'
loose over her and—and—well, give me what
you may call common appearances in females
—h'ordinary attractions, such as'll fit with
plain furniture and make a man feel home's
home."

"Well, I'm rather sorry to hear ye talkin'
like that," said Stone. "There's no harm
done, so far as I'm consarned, but your's
are sentiments which ye're likely to rap out
with ashore, an' it's just these here wulgar
notions which are helping to bring sailors
into scorn among landsmen. What d'ye
want with common appearances ? Why
should ye choose h'ordinary attractions? Ain't
sailors good enough for female beauty, that
they should make out they aren't by affectin'
a love for ugliness ? Don't talk to me, Bill,
about women as'll fit with plain furniture. As
an old sailor I'm for possessing what's most
beautiful an' desirin' of it for all my mates.
Let such notions as yours be thought the
feelin' of all sailors an' ye'd never get a really
nice-looking gal to look at a nautical man."

It was evident Breeches was rehearsing
some warm answer from the energetic manner

in which he mumbled his quid ; but fortun-
ately, perhaps for both old fellows, a hot
discussion was cut short by the arrival of
Hiram on deck.

In the cabin, Fortescue combing Agatha's
hair would have promised a wonderful study
to anyone looking on a minute or two ;
though much longer would it have needed to
witness the truth in the girl's quietness, the
passive clasp of her hands on her lap, the
listless steadfastness of the gaze that seemed
neither to see nor to heed anything.   Yet,
one would have been detained were it but for
the sake of her tranquil beauty, the shining
of her hair in the hands of her lover, his
gestures of tenderness, his side-long glances
at her, the radiance of passion that would
come floating into his large dark eyes,
replacing other expressions such as, particularly, the craving of anxiety.   The westering
sunshine broke in beams through the swaying
skylight, and went slipping like molten gold
along bulkhead and deck-floor ; the atmosphere trembled with the azure wind gushing
with sounds as of distant music in it down
through the lifted frames ; the splashing falls

of water over the side filled the ear with a
sense of refreshment. The beautiful hair
was wildly tangled indeed, yet it was bound
to yield to such gentle, loving, but resolute
handling as his. The touch of it! The
light upon it! Why, since it is known how
a little lock of the hair of the dead will move
the mourner, it is not hard to conceive what
sort of feelings came to the young clergyman
with the length of beaming tress he lifted—
the love unspeakable, the deep thanksgiving
to Almighty God for the guidance that had
brought this issue to pass ; yet both love and
gratitude interpenetrated by a sentiment of
secret consternation at the thought of the
blind, lustreless memory into whose darkness
he could peer without beholding the reflection
of the barest shadow of himself! So well as
he had been beloved too! Never had a
girl's heart been more wholly her lover's than
Agatha's. The ocean they had both loved,
whose spirit, hand in hand, they had often
sought to interpret, sitting or softly moving
upon the shore, when the summer afternoon blazed over the flashing mirror, or
when the moonlight rippled in the expanse

of silver dusk, how had it served them?
Dissevering them—filling the long interval
with anguish—uniting them again, but in
such wise that the poet's dream of death
in life seemed realised in the beauty of
the rescued girl, soulless in that past where
love was!

Well, it was inevitable that a hundred
such thoughts should pass through his mind,
as for an hour he stood combing her thick
hair into lengths of tresses, sometimes addressing her and obtaining rational and
gentle, drowsy answers.   At last his hand
ached, he could do no more, but he had
done much, the task was a practicable one,
and, by persevering, the tangled mass was
to be disciplined into its old rich auburn
silkiness.   She had evidently found a
pleasure in the caressing motion of his
hands.   When he dropped his task she
stood up, brought the hair he had smoothed
over her shoulder, and passing her fingers
through the silky golden length, smiled
with the happiness of a child.

"It is so much prettier thus," she
exclaimed, looking at it.   "It will be so

much more comfortable, too. But the combing of it all will take a long time."

"We have plenty of time," he answered.

She gazed at him as though she would thank him; but if that were her intention another thought or mood stole over and eclipsed it. Once again he noticed the slow wrinkling of her brows to a passage of bewilderment, which merely deepened to his own fixed regard, till the lifting of her hand to her forehead caused him to drop his eyes.

It was now tea-time. As she entered her berth Johnny arrived with the meal, and Archer turned out of his bunk. He saluted the clergyman and said, "I feel the better for that sleep, sir. But how a man dreams! I s'pose it was telling you my story that made me live all through that island job ag'in. It's puzzling, it's puzzling though," he exclaimed, rubbing his eyes. "When misfortunes comes to a man he thinks it's fancy till he grows used to it, and when he is out of troubles his release seems as much fancy as his misfortune was."

"Ay, and in my case, Archer, the wonder

in all that's happened since I parted with
Miss Fox in the Downs! The discovery of
the island! You, now, as you stand there
looking at me! All seems so visionary that
I could easily persuade myself I dreamt,
were it not for the grief her condition causes
me. That is too real for imagination! Tell
me, from the hour in which you discovered
that she lost her memory, did you ever detect
the least passing capacity in her to recall
incidents of her life before her recollection
went?"

"No, sir," Archer answered, thoughtfully.
"I tried her a many times, but found it was
like asking a person to peer into a dense fog
and say what was visible in it."

"You were very good to her, Archer;
most nobly humane and loyal," exclaimed
Fortescue, in a trembling voice.

"Sir," said the man, in a subdued, solemn
way, "the good God who was with her and
me on that island, and who brought your
honour to the rescue—He knows that if she'd
been my daughter I could not have done
more—acted otherwise than I did. I say it,
because I want ye to know the truth, to feel

the whole length of it along down to the very deepest it goes ; that is, to onderstand that Miss Fox comes to ye as she left you— an' this I says, speaking from my heart to God !"

His words did not need the almost sublime confirmation they found in the sheer English honesty of the earnest, rough, haggard, sailorly face. Once more Fortescue grasped his hand and held it in both his. Hiram came into the cabin.

" Well, Mr. Fortescue," he exclaimed, " an' how have ye managed with the lady's hair, sir ?"

" Very well. It needs time, but I shall manage."

" I shall be happy to take a spell at the combin' whenever you requires relievin'," said Hiram. " It don't ask, I suppose, for a more delikit hand than's wanted for unlayin' yarns for foxes or nettles for pointin ?"

Fortescue thanked him, and said he had no doubt he should be able to finish the combing without assistance. Archer was going.

"You'll stop and drink tea with us here?" said the clergyman.

"I'd rather not, thanking you all the same, sir. I'd sooner join the men in the fo'ksle. You'll put me in a watch, cap'n, I hope, and start me along with the crew. Don't reckon you'll find me much of a Dutchman, sir."

Hiram gave one of his neigh-like laughs. "Bo'sun of a H'indieman like the Werulam a Dutchman! Not yet, I hope, mister. The furriners is a-gatherin', and the British h'ensign might be the Royal Standard flying atop of the Tower o' Babel for the thunderin' number of tongues as are spoke under it. But the sarvice ain't altogether rotten yet. There's some parts free o' maggots, and I allow the Werulam was on the sweet-smellin' side of the cheese. Well, Archer——what's your t'other name by the way?"

"Henry."

"Well, then, Henry, subject to Mr. Fortescue's approval, what I says to you is, you can play or you can work; you can be man or you can be passenger; you can be put on the articles or you can sling a hammock and do nothen but smoke in it. You've had nine months of a lonely island, and arter such a spell of waitin' as that, why, if you ain't entitled to do jest whatever you best please, then let the world tarn to and call shipwreck a light diversion."

" I thank you, captain," said Archer, "but I'd rather do my bit, sir."

It was plain he felt he would be more comfortable among the men and working as a "hand," than living in the cabin and idling, and seeing this, Fortescue did not attempt to persuade him ; so with a flourish of his hand to his forehead the poor fellow took his leave and went forward.

"An honest man, that, sir," said Hiram.

" He is, and it is another proof of God's goodness that he should be so, Captain Weeks ; for think—had he been like the ruffian he struck down——" Fortescue shuddered violently. " What dreadful misery the sea heaps upon those whom it fixes on for its victims !" he continued. " Could one imagine such an experience to befall any lady on shore as to be boxed up for nine months with rough fellows—seamen—a class

of beings reckless at the best, but in suffering
often brutally and savagely heedless."

" Not all," observed Weeks, mildly.

" No, God forbid, not all," exclaimed Fortescue.

" Not nearly all," said Weeks, still mildly.

" Well, not nearly all," remarked the
clergyman.

" I'm not a man," said Hiram, " to say a
good word for them that's bad in my callin'.
Indeed, I'm rayther in favour of hangin' of
'em than excusin' of 'em—tho' I tell ye what,
sir, there's more excuses to be found for a
bad sailor than there is for a bad landsman ;
and that I'd wolunteer to prove at Exeter
Hall in the presence of any number of pious
noblemen, gentlemen, and ladies, if they'd
take the trouble to listen.   But when ye
come across a good man that's a sailor;
there's so much vartue in him that he carries
cargoes of principles in him enough for a
dozen.   So what I says is, one good sailor's
good enough to make a man willing to h'over-
look the evil in a score of his mates—jest as
ye taste a little dab of salt in a saucepanful of
vittles.   There ain't a bad word I'm ac-

quainted with forcible enough to fit that chap Stimson ; yet how many Stimsons do a man like Archer compensate the sarvice for ?"

He was interrupted by Agatha coming out of her berth. She came at once with a smile to Fortescue and said, " That is a wonderful box in my cabin. Everything I want is in it. I could not imagine how I should do up the hair you had combed out so that it should not mingle with the rest and become en-tangled again. I thought—and thought—and looked into the box and found what I should never have been able to ask for—a packet of hair-pins! Now see how I have managed," and turning her back upon her lover she let him observe that she had coiled the smooth tresses on her head, leaving the knotted mass still flowing down her shoulders.

" Ay, that will keep the tresses clear, and to-morrow we will have it all fairly combed out," exclaimed Fortescue, noticing, with a sud-den transport of hope and delight, her man-ner of approaching him, her ease in address-ing him, and, above all, the coherence and the rationality and the unhesitancy of her speech.

She asked for Archer ; the clergyman said

that at his own desire he had gone forward to take up his abode with the men.

"He is a sailor by profession," she said. "He told me he was the boatswain of the Verulam, an Indiaman that was burnt. I was on board of her, he has assured me, when the flames broke out, but," she added, with a singular touch of faint pettishness in her manner as she gazed with a soft glance that waned into listlessness even as Fortescue watched her, "he used to talk as if he knew me before I was born—or when I was some-body else. He made my head ache; but he was very, very kind, so gentle and thought-ful——"; her voice died away though her lips moved for some moments afterwards.

"I beg your pardon, ma'am," exclaimed Hiram, who had been staring at her with protruding eyes full of admiration and wonder and curiosity, "but might I make so bold as to ask if the h'idea of them there 'airpins you was a-tellin' Mr. Fortescue about, occurred to ye afore ye tarned to and sarched for them? For," added he, in a low voice, and in an aside to the clergyman, with an expression of countenance indicative of the most amiable willingness to assist in any way in restoring her memory, "if it did, it'll show recollection's a-breaking out."

The girl stared at him without answering, clearly not in the least comprehending him.

" I find it unwise to tax Miss Fox's memory at present," Mr. Fortescue said, in his kindest manner, and then he changed the subject by asking questions about the course, the speed, the time likely to be occupied in rounding the Cape, and so on.

They went on deck after the meal, and as the evening closed in upon them the sky became a dome of blazing gold, save in the furthest west where there lay a lagoon-like expanse of faint and tender green. The few clouds held the western flashing fair upon their brows as they looked sideways at the sinking luminary, whilst they floated into the north-west ; they seemed to echo the light on high, to reverberate the flying glory. The schooner was alone, the only object in the liquid circle that girdled an ocean like a heaving, glittering field of golden cloth ; her rigging had the burnished appearance of brass wire, her sails rose yellow, and gleaming over her, from truck to water-mark, the irradiation hung like a film, and you would have said she was sailing in an auriferous atmosphere of her own. Forward, the hands were assembled in a little crowd, listening to Archer who, seated on the windlass-end, talked with a sooty pipe between his teeth and his arms folded ; aft, the helm was grasped by James Kitt, who sent many a yearning glance from the binnacle to his mates on the forecastle, whilst Hiram patrolled the weather deck ; Stone, pipe in mouth, overhung the lee rail full of thought, and Fortescue and Agatha sat together gazing at the evening magnificence, and sometimes speaking.

But the old response was gone ! She looked as with new eyes at the visionary, fading splendour, at the gathering of the stars, at the noble and majestic appearance of the sky when every orb had kindled its fires of rose, or diamond, or blue in it. There was a time when she would have witnessed a poem in whatever her eye rested on, and found a melody for it by her expression of the meaning she beheld. Now—why, when

the night had descended dark and luminous,
with yellow glitterings in the sea-like mirror-
ings of the passage and breakings of the
meteors under the stars, he discovered no
chord in her to answer to a touch he might
have deemed sure, for to his reference of her
sense of the overwhelming mystery and loneliness of the night upon the island, with its
appalling environment of leagues of ocean,
she made no reply; she did not compre-
hend him ; he held her hand, but his words
put no such thrill in it as must have caused
it to tremble had she grasped his meaning,
and looked back and remembered the horror,
the feeling of desolation, the dreadful, heartbreaking hopelessness that would possess her
night after night when she stood alone, gazing seawards into the ebony distance, hearkening to the sullen booming of the surf on the
windward side and the complaining of the
wind among the bushes and the cocoa-nut
trees.   But all this was before her memory
went.   Since then, as he would perceive,
day and night were but the familiar conditions of her new intellectual birth, features
of her island-life which could breed no emo-

tion in her because from the blackness of the
past no associations could come to inform
them with impulses not their own.

Before two bells—nine o'clock—had been
struck she said she was sleepy.

" I always went to the house Archer built
for me and lay down soon after the sun had
set," she exclaimed.

He led her below, and entering her berth
saw that all was prepared for her, then
returned and took her hand.   He would
have taken her to his heart and kissed
her, but dared not for fear of frightening
her.

"God bless thee, my Agatha!   My precious
one !"

She smiled, coloured, drew her hand away,
said, "Good   night,   Mr.   Fortescue," and
entered her berth, but in an instant or two
after reappeared, holding her hand to her
forehead.

" I want to think," she said.

" Of what?   Tell me; I will think for you,"
he exclaimed.

There was a long silence.   "It is gone !"
she cried.   " It was—it was——" she shook

her head, the tears gushed into her eyes, she turned abruptly from her lover and closed the door of her berth upon herself.

CHAPTER II.

THE DREAMER.

IT was the first watch, and Stone had charge of it. Young Joe Hall held the tiller. The mate, observing Mr. Fortescue coming along to leeward, crossed the deck to see who it was.

"Why, sir, is it you? I thought you had turned in," he exclaimed.

"No, I have been alone on the forecastle for the last hour. This day has been fruitful, Mr. Stone—it has left me much to think of."

They came to the weather deck and began to walk.

"Yes, sir, it has been fruitful, as you say. I dunno that you could have used a better word—fruitful's the tarm. There's much not only to think of but to be thankful for. The woyage has answered its object. We've found and saved the lady, and another's life besides. It's been right all round — your wision, sir; my calkilations of the island; Hiram's navigation. It's been a marvellous bit of h'orderin', sir; everything so dove-tailing—you a-dreaming, me a-coming across your advertisement and knowing the island, Hiram steering straight for it, the lady alive and healthy, and an honest seaman left to look arter her. Why, what I says is, such a fitting of h'extraordinary sarcumstances, such a-combining of curiousist events, proves that the Creator's been in it, and that it's Him as has brought it all about. If that there notion don't go along with it, it'll be a yarn no un'll believe."

"At all events, we know it's real," said the clergyman, gently; "and to-day gives us faith in one another's sanity. It was not so before, I think. There was some mistrust, but the truth is now known, and how grateful I feel towards you, Mr. Stone, for your noble sincerity, for your sailorly sympathy——-"

The old fellow interrupted: "Don't thank me, sir; we've all done our bit—mine's nothen worth noticing. There's no doubt Hiram got to think me inventive, as if I'd fancied myself cast away and imagined the island, and believed in it as gospel through mere keepin' all on repeatin' of it. But that's past. Next job's the lady. She'll get her memory yet; I do believe it, sir."

Mr. Fortescue was silent.

"It's perhaps a pity," continued Stone, "that ye didn't bring your uniform along with you—I mean the clargyman's garments as may be she was used to seeing you in. If you was to put them on perhaps she'd know you!"

"No," said Mr. Fortescue, thoughtfully, "if she does not know me by my face she would not know me by my professional dress."

"Well, perhaps so, sir; but it's putting a lot of things together as makes a likeness. Take a familiar member o' royalty and see him stripped to his drawers—no cocked hat on, no h'orders, no uniform; nothen but drawers. Ye would not believe it possible, Mr. Fortescue! Arter the likeness of him, you'd look an' say, 'No, that ain't the royalty what hangs in the winders.'"

The clergyman laughed, which encouraged

Stone in his garrulity, for the old fellow dearly loved a talk; besides, it was a long stretch of watching, from eight to midnight, with nothing to do but nod at the stars.

"It was only the other day, sir, that you was speakin' to me about Miss Fox's health, wonderin', if you found her at all, how she'd have worn. That speculation's ended, sir; but it's the queerest part of the whole soopernat'ral business. She leaves England ill, she gets cast away upon an island, and arter nine months ye find her healthier than ever she was, and the picture of beauty, as the sayin' is."

"Archer's explanation I believe to be the true one," answered Mr. Fortescue, "and it shows him possessed of a very great deal of sagacity and intelligence to hit upon it. The state of one's health is greatly dependent upon the mind. Half the pains, sicknesses, aches of this life, come through persons dwelling upon themselves. Whilst Miss Fox's memory was sound she fretted incessantly and wasted away, as Archer told us. But when her memory went her grief disappeared, nothing lingered for her heart to

sadden over; she looked forth upon a new
life—an existence without regrets, without
bereavements, without remembrances; upon a
universe of ocean and sky, from whose
enriching qualities of sunshine and breeze
she would receive the same tonical spirit that
gave beauty and colour and fertility to the
green growths of the island—her little world!
It is as Archer suggested; between her and
health, between her youth and nature, there
stood nothing when her memory went. "Ah!"
he cried, clasping his hands convulsively, "I
could believe it was for the best, as have
been all things, did I dare hope her memory
would come back to her."

"For my part," said Stone, keeping pace
with a deep-sea roll to Mr. Fortescue's
strides, "I don't see how it can be helping
of it. The look-out 'ud be a bad 'un, I
dessay, if her recollection was clean gone; if
she couldn't remember what she'd say a
moment arter sayin' of it; if she wasn't to be
trusted to tarn in by herself or to be alone in
her berth; but when ye see her h'acting in
such a way that if a man didn't know her
memory stopped dead short a few months

past——why! Gracious mussy, Mr. Fortescue, here she is, sir! Lord, the turn she's
given 'me!"

He was close to the companion-hatch as
she rose slowly out of it, and so startling was
the effect of her unexpected apparition upon
him that he recoiled by several steps with a
grip of the arm of his companion that
dragged the clergyman with him. The
moon had risen to add a little brilliancy to
the soft and sifting effulgence of the stars.
The white decks, the white canvas, helped
the sheen, and, as Agatha stepped off the
companion-ladder, disclosing her whole figure,
Mr. Fortescue could see she had robed herself in the gown she had been wearing during
the day, but her feet were bare and her head
uncovered. The clergyman was about to
spring forward, but something in her manner
struck him; he trembled violently to the
sudden curbing of his emotions and to the
suspicion that had flashed upon him.

"Hush!" he whispered to Stone, raising
his hand.

The girl advanced by two or three paces
towards the helm, halted and inclined her

face to left and right several times, as though seeking some object out upon the sea. Mr. Fortescue stole to her side and looked at her. Her eyes were wide open, and even in that faint light he could witness so much vitality in her face that ere he could satisfy himself that she was actually walking in her sleep he found it necessary to stand right in front of her that the slumberous blindness of her staring eyes might be proved. Being satisfied, he crept back to Stone and said, in a whisper, "She is walking in her sleep."

" Ha!" exclaimed the old fellow, pulling off his cap and wiping his forehead, but speaking in a tone that showed his courage had returned to him. "She mustn't be woke, sir—best to let that there trick have its way, I've always heard."

"But her feet are bare, Mr. Stone—she is insufficiently clothed—the dew is heavy," said Mr. Fortescue, brokenly, in a torment of un-certainty of purpose.

"She'll not hurt, sir; consider how she's been exposed, how used she is to it, and how a special providence watches over sleep-walkin'," said Stone. "For the Lord's sake don't wake her; the fright might do her cruel harm."

"See, she is moving again! Be by my side, Mr. Stone! I may lose my nerve if I should have to act suddenly."

She went to the taffrail, Mr. Fortescue and Stone following within grasp of her. The man, Joe Hall, at the helm, judging how it was with her by the behaviour of the curate and the mate, slipped like lightning to the other side of the tiller that it might be between him and her, and then stood transfixed, staring at her till his dilated eyes looked like white blots upon his shadowed face. God knows how it was, but even to her lover, her blind, unknowing, unconscious presence put an element of wild mystery into the beauty of the night. The singing of the wind in the rigging came down with a hollower note of complaint; there was a sound of sobbing in the plashing of the water alongside; it seemed to him that the very stars beyond her, over the sea-line, dimmed their sparkles into a sober wanness, and that the dark shadow of the wide deep grew spectral through the mere sense of the sharper chill the wind swept off its glooming heart.

She stood for at least a minute at the taff-rail with her hands folded, apparently gazing into the distant gloom over the stern.

"What has caused this?" muttered the clergyman to Stone. "It can be no habit of hers. Archer would have mentioned it, for he was sure to have detected it."

"It may be the excitement of the day," said Stone, hoarsely.

"Ay, some inward perturbation master-ing her—perhaps memory, her imprisoned memory, acting upon what, when she is awake, keeps it bound down and paralysed, but which, being weakened by sleep, yields to the struggling faculty. Great heavens! How wonderful is the human spirit! It was the deep agitation produced by my vision that caused me to walk in my sleep. I had never done so before—have never done so since. Poor girl—my own beloved! Oh! it must be as you say, Mr. Stone—the excitement of the day acting upon her through the memory that lives when she sleeps!"

He yearned to clasp her, to gather her to

the warmth of his arms and his heart. It
was unbearable to see her standing bare-
footed, bareheaded—so lonely, so lonely as
she looked, abstracted from all things by
sleep, the brother of death, more startling
even than death in this blank, mocking,
almost unmeaning trick of it.

She sighed deeply and turned; they stepped
away and she passed them. She now began
to pace the deck from the taffrail to a little
before the mainmast, walking slowly and with
a singular regularity of gait, her hands hanging idly by her side, her head bowed as
though she gazed fixedly down, her attitude
that of one profoundly engrossed by thought.
They followed her close for fear of some
impulse seizing her, some behaviour that
would demand instant checking. It was a
time and a sight to make a bold man hold his
breath and yet feel quit of cowardice too.
Every circumstance heightened in dramatic
intensity this act of somnambulism. The
masses of the girl's rough hair streamed
meteor-like down her back, or were shaken by
the breeze; the velvet tread of her naked feet
gave her movements the gliding character

the superstitious mind loves to believe peculiar to the motions of spectres and apparitions ; her face was like a star in the luminous gloom, but, to Mr. Fortescue's gaze, with the wonder of death-in-life in it, owing to its immobility and to the mockery of the sightless eyes counterfeiting the intent regard of wrapt sensibility. Softly to and fro, close behind her, the clergyman and Stone followed; the wind swept a hundred sounds of crying voices through the rigging, the schooner leaned under the weight in her canvas, and the white water swept past into a long wake giddy with dim green glitterings.

Presently Agatha stopped, looked again as before from right to left, from left to right, and then going to the lee rail put her hands upon it and so stood, seemingly gazing over the bulwarks at the junction of sea and sky that was definable only by the vanishment of the stars where the ocean was. Stone, at a gesture from Mr. Fortescue, posted himself close on her left, the clergyman on her right. Thus guarded from herself she was safe. After a little she began to speak.

"Malcolm!" she exclaimed, distinctly, and

in a voice of fretful misery, "do you never mean to seek me? I think of you day and night, day and night! Have you forgotten me? You loved me deeply—I know you did. Remember, dearest, your words to me when you said farewell on the Verulam. Am I so far away that you will not seek me? Were the grave between us I would pray for death that I might join you. Oh! Malcolm, it is hard to be left to this fearful solitude—this dreadful loneliness! Hush! the sound of the surf is like a perpetual cursing of me by the ocean. Malcolm! Malcolm! do you never mean to seek me?"

Her voice to this rose shrill, and she clasped her hands and lifted her face.

"Answer her, sir," muttered Stone, behind his hand; "there's memory here."

"I am coming, I have come, Agatha," said Mr. Fortescue, instantly grasping the old man's idea, yet starting at the sound of his own voice and trembling under the emotion of awe her speech and his answering her filled him with.

"But you are still far away—at Wyloe. You are standing in the porch of the church,

looking at me—thinking of me! Oh, come—
come to me!" She flung forth her arms in
the exact posture of entreaty he had seen her
assume in his vision.

"Keep her to her memory, sir; work at
it! It may produce what's a-missin'," said
Stone, again behind his hand, in a whisper
hoarse with excitement.

She was dreaming; her lover saw that.
He was visible to her soul's eye, and her soul
was addressing him. That memory was not
dead in her would be proved if it could be
seen that it operated like an active principle
in her when intellectual vitality was purely
spiritual in its conditions. Her lover felt the
need of farther testing this, but awe rendered
the obligation hard, and the deep tenderness
of his human love felt upon it the chill
of that preternatural converse, as though,
addressing one that was dead, he found
himself answered.

"Come to me!" she repeated, in a fainter
voice, bringing her hands to her bosom and
clasping them.

"Do not you hear me tell you I am
coming, my own?" he said.

"Yes, I hear you," she replied, gazing straight out to sea.

"Where are you?"

"On an island—in the Indian Ocean—alone with a seaman. Oh, God! how many months have I passed in this dreadful solitude? Come to me, come to me!"

"I am coming, I am coming, my beloved! But, Agatha, why is it that you are on the island?"

"The Verulam was burnt at sea; many of us were crowded into one boat; we sickened of thirst and hunger, and several men died; till this island arose, and then we were dashed by the surf upon it!"

"Great mercy!" whispered Stone behind his hand, "think o' that! If her memory was a bell it couldn't be sounder."

She slightly inclined her head as if listening; in every syllable that fell from her lips there was a singular thrilling sound like the vibration in a bar of silver after it has been struck; meanwhile she kept her face steadfastly directed seawards, so that the impression conveyed by this fixed posture to Mr. Fortescue and the mate was that she actually beheld him she was answering upon the darkness there, God alone knows how far off.

" Is Dr. Clayton with you ?"

" No—we were separated by the crowds rushing to the boats."

" Will you be glad to see me, my own ?"

" Oh, my darling, come to me, come to me !" she cried, in a voice of exquisite sweetness.

" Will you remember me when we meet ?"

" Remember thee !" she replied, lapsing in this answer into the tender Quaker speech she used sometimes, in moments of lightheartedness, to reply to or address him at Wyloe. " I am looking at thee, Malcolm ; thine eyes are sad, thy face hollow. Thou hast been grieving for me, Malcolm. Remember thee ! Oh ! come—come—come !" Again she extended her hands and convulsive sobs broke from her.

For some minutes after he was silent she remained in her former intent, staring, and hearkening attitude ; she then sighed deeply, quitted the bulwarks, took some turns along the deck, again walked to the bulwarks and looked and listened as before, and with another heart-broken sigh glided to the companion-hatch and went below. The clergyman followed, whispering good-night to Stone. She made straight to her berth and closed the door after her; he waited a little, then opened the door, softly withdrew the key, and turned the lock from the outside, leaving the key in the lock that it might be instantaneously used if needed. This done, he withdrew to his own little berth, where, being hidden from all sight but God's, he cast himself down in a chair in a bitter fit of weeping that was good for him, for the relief to his overcharged heart was like the easing of some strangling pain; and with a cleansed brain he could pray, and think clearly of what had passed.

CHAPTER III.

FORTESCUE passed a broken night. He could hardly close his eyes for deep, anxious and bewildering thoughts. All the mystery and awe of his own vision and its astonishing accomplishment were, now that the issue was reached, now that Agatha was safe, overshadowed by the wonder of the extraordinary psychological conundrum that the shipwreck of his beloved had confronted him with. Would it, as he had more than once thought in the day that had passed, come to his having to build up a fresh fabric of emotion on her new faculty of recollection, win her love this side the veil that had fallen, and teach her heart afresh all those former passions and delights which had found a grave in her memory?

He awoke at half-past seven, and after

gently turning the key in Agatha's door, and
listening, he went on deck, where he found
Hiram and Stone walking up and down, the
watch below coming to the caboose for their
breakfast, the watch on duty clearing up the
decks, and a strong wind blowing from the
southward, yet without much sea. The sky
was a dingy blue, and the scud was flying
along it like the scatterings of the sooty
belchings of a city of factory chimneys
behind the windward ocean. The Golden
Hope was rushing through it with flattened
sheets and single-reefed mainsail; the water
poured in a white arch from the weather bow,
and the heel of her as she shredded the surges
wonderfully accentuated the idea of swift
motion indicated by the whirling passage of
the creaming stuff to leeward, whose seething the wind echoed in screams as it tore
bucketsfull of it up and drove the blobs like
chips of glistening white coral into the air.

It was a fine, rushing picture to come
upon from a small cabin; and it was the
heartier as a vitalising influence because of
the feeling that the schooner was homeward
bound. Weeks and Stone touched their

caps as the curate approached them ; there
was some talk of the weather, the rate of
sailing, the promise of a speedy passage
home and the like, then said Fortescue :—

"I suppose, captain, Mr. Stone has told
you what happened last night?"

"He did, sir, at h'eight bells when I come
on deck. We took the liberty of talkin' about
it, perhaps for half-an-hour, sartinly not less
I should think, Bill? For, remarkable as
your wision was, sir, I can't but consider it's
amaziness clean swamped by this here sleep-
walkin' an' recollectin'. Think of a gent
stanning alongside a lady an' she a-talkin' to
him as if he wur ten thousand mile off—sound
asleep, too, for all her *col*-lected h'answering!
Tell ye what it is, Mr. Fortescue, this here
woyage makes one see there's more inside of
a chap than it might be h'agreeable to him to
know he's got, if his narves ain't as well set
up as a line-o'-battle ship's lower riggin'. I
mean to give up doubtin', myself. It must be
an out-and-out twister as 'ud cause me to call
a man a liar for tellin' of it."

"Is Archer on deck?" said Fortescue.
"I wish to ask him a question."

Old Stone sang out, and, with man-of-war-like smartness, Archer sprang through the forescuttle and stepped aft. He gave the old-fasioned marine scrape of that day, and stood, tall, erect, respectful, waiting to be addressed, an excellent sample of the English mariner. In his gentle, cordial, sympathetic way, Fortescue inquired after his health, how he had rested, and so forth, and then said :—

"Archer, during the time you were on the island with Miss Fox did you ever know her to walk in her sleep?"

"No, sir."

"Do you feel sure that she never did?"

"Well, sir, of course when I was sleeping myself I couldn't know what she did; but I never imagined it, I never suspected it, and I don't think she did."

"I am asking because she walked last night; Mr. Stone and I guarded her, and I asked her questions to which she responded with perfect clearness of memory—questions referring to what she does not recollect when she is awake."

"I think, sir," said Archer, "if it was her custom I should have found it out."

That was all Fortescue required to know and Archer went forward.

"Beg your pardin', sir," said Stone, with hesitation mixed with the tone his voice took from the profound interest he felt in the matter, "but don't you like the idea of the lady walkin' in her sleep, sir?"

"No."

"But," continued the old man, "don't you fancy, sir, that these here conversations with you in her sleep might come to make an impression upon her as a dream which some fine mornin' she'd wake up and recollect?"

"Dunno if Mr. Fortescue understands ye, Bill," exclaimed Hiram, "but bile me if I do, mate."

"Why," grumbled Stone, sourly, "how would ye have any livin' man put it better? Call it me—I ain't got no memory; I walks in my sleep, dreams an' answers questions. Werry good. What I says is, one mornin' I wakes up and says to myself, I says, 'Gor bless me! last night I dreamt o' so and so'— things, look ye, Hiram, I couldn't recollect of afore when I was awake, and in that way mem'ry retarns. D'ye understand now?"

" Why, yes," responded Hiram, with a dull, protruding gaze at the sea astern, " I see what ye're a-trying to drive at ; but I don't think it 'ud answer—that is if you wants my opinion."

" Anyway, Mr. Fortescue," exclaimed Stone, " if I was you, sir, I'd encourage that sleep-walkin' in the lady. Leastways, seeing that it's a habit, I shouldn't worrit over her a-practisin' of it. If it hadn't been for *your* walkin' and dreamin' she wouldn't be aboard !"

And squinting at Hiram with a triumphant glitter in his eye over this stroke, he suddenly appeared to find something wrong with the set of a headsail, and strode forward, calling out.

It is scarcely conceivable that Fortescue should attach much significance to the metaphysical theories of such men as Stone and Captain Weeks. A knowledge of the medicinal and fortifying properties of old Jamaica rum, intimate acquaintance with shipboard duties, the art of setting up rigging, of taking a vessel to pieces and putting her together again ; these things were to be ex-

pected in two such seasoned "lobscousers;
but when it came to their notions of the
operation of the soul and the movements of
the human understanding under strained and
singular conditions, why, there was a laugh
to be got out of their talk, no doubt, but
very little in the shape of an idea.

And yet, as the curate followed with his
eye the rolling figure of old Stone striding
towards the forecastle, it seemed to him that
there might be something, too, in the seaman's fancy that dreams such as Agatha
dreamt last night, deepened by his questions,
might recur to her on waking and bring with
them recollections of the things the visions
concerned. The fancy, or rather the hope
affected him; he went below, and finding the
door still closed lightly tapped upon it. It
was immediately opened. The girl was fully
dressed in her attire of yesterday. He
grasped her hand with a moment's pause ere
speaking, not knowing what expression her
face might take to the meeting of their eyes;
but it needed only a moment, and he bade
her good-morning with a voice that faltered
with a passing sickness of heart.

"I was this instant coming on deck, Mr. Fortescue," said she, smiling as she inclined her head. "It is a cosy little bedroom," glancing around her; "but the deck gives me the space I enjoyed on the island. I love movement and I like to see the wide sky all around me. It is a habit—it may have been so before my memory went."

She sighed lightly, and looked down upon the deck with a grave face, as though she talked of the dead or something that demanded a solemnity in her. He noticed that she was a shade paler than he had observed her to be on the previous day. He could not be sure that it was not owing to the fainting of the island's sunny glow on her face. In the schooner she was protected from the tropical glare by awnings, sails, and decks; and it was to be expected that the delicate tinge which, combined with her disordered masses of shining hair, rendered her free, developed beauty—bright as ocean light, healthful as ocean wind—almost startling for the singularity of its charms, should yield to the natural velvet whiteness of her skin; otherwise there was nothing to indicate that she suffered in any respect from her exposure during the night, or from whatever mental sufferings her dreaming had excited in her.

" Did you sleep well ?"

" Very well."

" Did no sounds on deck, no movement of the schooner disturb you ? No sense of the novelty of a bed after your island house of leaves—no dreams ?" he exclaimed with a forced smile, eager to touch her memory, yet not wishing that she should find his manner suggestive of his desire.

She shook her head and answered: "Nothing. I slept soundly." She then came into the cabin from the doorway of her berth, and, putting her hand against a stancheon, appeared to notice for the first time the jumping and swinging motion of the vessel. She was clearly giving it her mind, whilst she kept her soft eyes fastened thoughtfully upon the clergyman, and in a moment or two she said, " This swinging feeling is familiar to me ; it brings back— What ? What ?" and as she spoke a sudden gleam of fear shone in her glance.

He waited to see if more would dawn upon

her, but observing the old glazing expression
to creep over her face, he exclaimed with a
passionate anxiety to quicken what appeared
to be a dim stirring in her, "It reminds you
of the Verulam, Agatha—of the heave of
the great ship upon the billows. Can you
recollect now?"

"No," she answered, in a tone of weariness,
"I cannot remember, I cannot remember,
Mr. Fortescue," and she raised her eyes to
his with an extraordinary look of pathetic,
wistful entreaty as if she was in dread that
she would be chided. With an effort of
powerful determination he changed his
manner and put a note of lively heartiness
into it.

"We shall be having breakfast in half-an-
hour," said he; "instead of our going on deck
let me comb some more of these pretty
tresses. I long to see them in shining coils
upon your head, for the sake of your comfort,
and for their preservation."

She laughed and acquiesced, and removed
the seal-skin cap. In a few moments he
was at work, pausing often to caress her
head and hair, bringing the lengths to one

or the other side of her that he might see
her face.

By the time breakfast was served, he had
made such good headway with the combing
job that another hour spent upon her hair
would give it back its old smooth, silken
beauty in completeness. He remarked that
as Captain Weeks came below his long gaunt
bow to her had a touch of timidity in it, and
that he cast several askant looks at her after
they were seated. In truth, her sleep-walking
had weighed more upon Hiram than he
cared to admit. But he had a bit of news
to relate ; so in a sort of bustling way, as
though to overwhelm the agitation he felt
on finding himself close to the mysterious,
beautiful girl who answered questions in her
sleep and could talk to her lover all the way
to Wyloe from the middle of the Indian
Ocean, "and him 'longside her all the time,"
as he had said to Stone, he exclaimed :
" There's a steamer's smoke on the weather
quarter, Mr. Fortescue. She'll be a steamer
—not a wessel on fire—for the place where
the smoke's a-comin' from is travellin' as fast
as we are."

" It's strange to meet a steamer hereabouts
—so few as they are," said Fortescue.

" Why, it sartinly is. 'Tain't to be supposed she's been sent on our arrant, for who's
to know that any surwivors of the Werulam
was cast away upon Stone's Island—onless
she's been commissioned to sarch these
waters.   Yet it's odd, too, she should be in
the neighbourhood of that there island—
'ceptin' if sarchin's her errand they've took
a plaguey long time to make up their
minds."

" It might be," exclaimed Fortescue, much
excited by these surmises, " that some of the
Verulam's people have reached India, and
that this steamer has been despatched from
Bombay or Calcutta, or any other port where
the news of the wreck was first received, to
visit the islands in these seas !"

" Well, we shall see," said Hiram.   " Any-
ways the smoke to wind'ard's a steamer's.
Only suppose she should be a h'enemy ?
Suppose war's broke out between Great
Britain and some furrin' country—France or
the United States !"   He drew a long face.
" By golly, Mr. Fortescue, there's never no

tellin'. We've been three months h'absent,
an' in three months there's plenty o' time for
a all-round shindy big enough to drive the
Proosians into H'asia Miney and to enable
the Sooltan of all the Turkeys to pray to his
Prophet in St. Patrick's Cathedral. A pretty
bloomin' affair now it 'ud be to be taken
prisoners!" And one could see that the
long-legged, hollow-cheeked fellow was perfectly sincere in the alarm he was kindling in
himself, by the hurried way he masticated his
food and tossed down his coffee.

To all this Agatha paid no attention whatever. Sometimes Fortescue would observe
her looking at him with an air of meditation
that his hope accepted as a manifestation of
inward struggle, till he'd see that it was no
more than an interest he was exciting in her,
and that she was comparing him with Hiram,
and with Archer, perhaps, and Stone. This,
to be sure, he could only imagine, for in her
darkened mind even her own eye would fail
to follow the movements of her thoughts; yet
he might be right, and it was certain at least,
that as her lover, as Malcolm Fortescue of
Wyloe, as her betrothed, her memory con-

fronted him as blank and blind as the stare
of a corpse.

Hiram had made himself uncomfortable,
and after a hasty breakfast ran on deck
with a glass to watch the steamer. There
was nothing, indeed, remarkable in his mis-
giving, unless it were its prematureness.
Those were days when France was like a
boil on Europe, keeping the whole body
politic irritable. There was also a tendency
on the part of Jonathan and John Bull to
throw themselves into sparring attitudes,
spite of the vast amount of soothing syrup
that was talked to allay the spasms of the
press on both sides ; in short, even at home,
a man never knew what a day might bring
forth, and a skipper, therefore, who had been
three months at sea without speaking an
outward ship and obtaining a word of news,
scarcely deserved ridicule for throwing an
alarmed glance at anything resembling a
pursuit, especially when it made a smoke.

Fortescue waited for Stone to arrive for
his breakfast before conducting Agatha on
deck. The old chap came bundling down
in a hurry and fell to eating in hot haste.

"Is the steamer still in sight?" asked the clergyman.

"Ay, sir; a good deal too much in sight," responded the mate, with his mouth full. "It's sartin she's twigged us and has shifted her helm, for her canvas is rising fast."

"But surely," exclaimed Fortescue, much disquieted by Stone's impetuosity, and hurry, and manner, "there is nothing to alarm one in that, is there? She may wish to speak us."

"Yes," said Stone, as drily as earnest mastication would permit, "h'exactly, sir. That's jest no doubt what he do want. But why? And who is he? I mean what's his flag? And what is he a-doin' down here?" And the old fellow wagged his head most portentously, whilst the steady grinding of his jaws behind his closed mouth gave a ripe curl of sourness to his lips each time they met.

When Fortescue conducted Agatha on deck he was surprised to notice on the weather quarter, where nothing had been visible when he went below, the smoke and canvas of a steamer that was obviously making a freer wind of it than the schooner. She was under a press of sail, and the cloths came

out in a froth-like white against the dark slate
of the masses of flying vapour that way, so
resembling the melting of the heads of the
seas into snow it was puzzling to tell one
from the other; the smoke flew back in a
long trail down upon the water, and it was
plain that the vessel, whatever she might be,
was sweeping through it at a very great pace.
Hiram was working away at her with the
telescope as though he would drive the one
protruding eye he looked with sheer into the
tube.

"I dunno, I'm sure, what to make of her,"
he exclaimed, turning his long, gaunt face,
that literally twitched and crawled with per-
plexity and bother, to the curate. "She's
rigged as a three-masted schooner, and's got
a foreroyal, and it's set. Has h'every appearance of a gun-boat. What's she a doing of
here? It's clear she's headin' for us. What's
to be done? If it was evening instead of
morning I'd hook it, take count o' the night
and chance the rest. As it is——" he paused,
with an eager, restless, stare aloft and then
a long look at the growing canvas to windward.

" But she may be a countryman of ours, Captain Weeks."

" Ay, but supposin' she ain't, sir ?"

" She is certain to hoist her colours."

" Yes, but suppose war's broke out, who's a-goin' to trust to bunting ? She may be a furriner and yet run the English ensign aloft jest to make sure of us by our answer. Damme—beg pardon, I'm sure—but what I mean is—damme if I know what to do !"

Here old Stone arrived.

" Every minute's·lettin' her gain upon us, Bill," cried Hiram to him. " By pilin' on, th' Hope ought to be able to make an all day chase of it, with this here breeze, spite of his enjines. Take the glass and tell us if there's anything ye can find noticeable in her."

Stone put the telescope on the rail and curved his shell-shaped back to it.

" She's a man-o'-war," he exclaimed, suddenly, springing erect and turning with an emphatic manner.

" Ye think so ?"

" Onmistakable. There's a hoist and a trim and a cut and a look I'd swear to if I had to pay the wages of this here woyage for proving wrong. Likely enough to be a British gun-boat."

"And likely as not to be some blasted furriner!" cried Hiram, forgetting his manners in his excitement and alarm. "Out with this reef, Bill! Friend or h'enemy, we've no call to wait for him. Lads, tumble aft here and shake this reef out. Hi, you, Johnny! jump aloft and loose the t'gallan's'l! Harry," putting his hand to his mouth to bawl to Sawyer, who was smoking a pipe in the head, "sing out to Bill an' Martin and t'others to come up and set the squaresail. Let her go off, Jimmy! two full points—you have her! William," addressing Stone, "see them head-sheets eased off. Look alive, lads. We'll want stunsails on her in a minute! Whoop! the old gal feels the wind when the choke of its grip is off her," and he slapped his knees with both hands, producing a sound like the report of a pistol as he peered to leeward at the water that spun by like boiling milk, rising in foam to the figure-head and bursting away from either bow in steaming clouds as the shifting of the helm enabled the clipper to take the fuller weight of the strong wind into the iron-hard hollows of her thunderous canvas.

The men, not understanding what was the matter, but smelling danger in all this commotion, ran about as for their lives. The fact is, there was something really contagious in Hiram's alarm, and at such times few men stop to reason. Even to Fortescue, the schooner's canvas, mounting like a growing light against the liftings of the sombre clouds, took a malignant character, though he could not have said why. Hiram came to him whilst the men were pulling and tumbling about, and after a look at the steamer under the sharp of his hand, cried out as though he were talking to himself:—

"Ay, she may be, but who's to know? And when known, if it don't prove correct, why, of course, then it's too late. If she's an Englishman, *I* don't want to run away. Not likely. But how's a man to guess? Not by the flag she'll hoist. No; if she's an enemy, if there's war, if her game be to nab all she can come across, she'll up with any colour that to her fancy may resemble our own flag, jest to bamboozle us and bring us within range by lullin'

suspicion. But she ain't going to lull *me !*"
he shouted, with a jump that nearly tumbled
him on to his nose. " Mr. Stone, git that
topmast stunsail-boom rigged out and the sail
set. Show yourselves alive, bullies ! Why,"
he bawled, "there may be a Roosian, or a
French, or a Yankee prison inside that there
hooker yonder !"

It was plain that the fears excited by the
heaving into view of the steamer had got a
firm hold of Hiram's mind.

"See here, sir!" he exclaimed, turning
rapidly upon Fortescue, and pouring out his
words with pell-mell haste and an argumenta-
tive tone in them: "We've been three
months h'absent ; there may be war ; at the
present moment Britain may be fightin' with
God knows what nations ; that steamer may
be an enemy ; we, not suspecting, heaves-to,
a boat arrives, and, by the Lord, afore we can
sing out, here we are clapped under hatches,
a prize crew aboard, and a chap with a moustache a-heading the Golden Hope for a
neutral port. Why not? Ain't it possible?
What 'ud be the good of heaving-to in order
to make sure when what I says is all pos-

sible ?   Think I want to be locked up?
Wessel taken from me ?   Nothen to receive?
The port o' London, where I belongs, as
wisionary as the island was when you dreamt
about it in your willage?"

He ran to the lee side to stare at the foam
sweeping past, then rushed up to the weather
quarter again, and, picking up the telescope,
levelled it at the steamer.   He looked at her
for some moments ; Fortescue watched him.
Suddenly he dropped the glass and turned an
ashen face upon the curate.

"Good God!" he gulped, as though he
swallowed whilst he spoke the words.

"What is it?" demanded Fortescue, now
rendered thoroughly nervous by the man's
consternation.

" Bill!" yelled Hiram.

Old Stone came rolling along as fast as he
could stir his legs.

" He's set topmast and t'gall'n-stunsails.
Bill!" cried Hiram, pointing to the steamer
with the telescope.

" He's arter us, then !" said Stone.

" He's headin'," continued Hiram, "broad
off, actually quarterin' the wind !   And why?

To get to loo'ward of us, where his engines'll let him have it all his own way if so
be as he can jam us when there into a ratch."

"Give us hold of the glass," cried Stone,
who had grown a shade or two paler also.
There was a pause; the old fellow brought
his eye away from the telescope. "Ay, he's
arter us! His game's as you say—to get to
loo'ward of us! It don't look friendly—it
don't look friendly. An' he's overhauling us.
Yes," taking another look, "there's no mis-
takin'; he's going through it faster nor we
are. Steam and sail combined must out-
weather us! Well, here's a pretty mess to
come all the ways into the H'injie Ocean to
tumble into!"

CHAPTER IV.

THE wind was what a sailor would term a topgallant breeze, with weight enough in it to single reef the topsails for a prudent skipper; and under the wide spread of cloths which Hiram's alarm had flung upon his vessel the schooner was driving along like a racehorse at a finish.

Agatha had seated herself on the low skylight whilst Fortescue talked with the captain, and there she remained, watching the men making sail and looking around her, doubtful, timid, wondering, at first startled by Hiram's excited orders and the hoarse and roaring "Cheerly men!" chorus at the halliards and wherever a pull was taken, and by the rushing noises of the passing waters on either hand, and the faint thunder of pouring billows, and the screaming and wailing as of a thousand fifes and bagpipes in the rigging, till the whole spirit of the thing coming into her, mainly as one might suspect through the buoyant leapings and floating rushings and shootings of the hull and the increased speed of it, she sprang to her feet with a brilliant flush in her cheeks and the light of the sudden gladness and deep excitement of her heart in her eyes, and, with amazing grace and nimbleness, leapt on to the bulwark rail and there stood, with her arm round a back-stay, gazing out to sea, away on the weather bow, her dress rattling like a flag, her hair blowing inboard—for the whole mass of it lay on her back again—her figure leaning well away, and an air of triumph on her face that was like the radiance of mirth without expression of laughter.

Plenty of notice would at any other time have been given to her by the crew, who reckoned her crazy and fearsome in other ways, for Joe Hall had carried forward all the news about her sleep-walking, though the men had had no time to talk the thing over, but their attention was fixed on the steamer astern. They stood all together near the weather forerigging, speculating upon the vessel's nationality, and most of them as alarmed as Hiram himself.

"I 'spose the skipper understands what he's about," said the cook. "He's bin long enough at sea to know what o'clock it is. You may reckon, lads, that something invisible to us has taken his h'eye or he'd never sweat th' old hooker in this fashion."

"Well, it'll be a pretty bloomin' look-out for us if so be she tarns out an enemy," exclaimed Breeches. "He's bound to have us. His manoover's quite plain. He's stealing to loo'ard and means to jam us with his bloomin' machinery. Well, if there's war and she's a h'enemy, it's good-night. I've heard what furrin jails is like, and the black bread they feed ye on, an' any man who's got a wife had better make up his mind to start a new home when he comes out, for starvation'll have given him another face, I allow. His friends won't know him, and any boots he may have left ashore he'll find filled up with another man's feet. I'm aweer of what I'm talkin' about. There was Billy Smithers. He wor captured out of a H'indieman somewhere up here. When he was liberated he found his wife had been twice married since him, and the chap as was then coortin' her 'broke Billy's head as an impostor."

He sent a gloomy look over the taffrail and folded his arms with a stare at the cook's pale face. Johnny, the boy, began to blubber.

" For this here schooner to be taken and us men made prisoners of 'll be a pleasin' tarmination of the woyage, sartinly," said Goldsmith, in a growling ironical voice, and savagely burying his hands in his pockets. "I know I wish I'd never shipped. Don't believe I ever should if it hadn't been for Duck parsuadin' of me. There's that about this here woyage that's kep' me uncomfortable all through. Why, damme, I wouldn't half so much object to the parson's wision if it hadn't turned out true. It's its trueness as disagrees with me. If a man points to a corner and says 'There's the Devil,' and there's nothen there, I laugh at him; but if he points and I look and sees a black man with a tail 'twixt his legs and eyes as big as

riding-lights, why then, ye see, I wants to
retire. There's a sight too much of what
ain't natural in this woyage. Don't want to
say nothen against the lady, but if Joe ain't
telling lies when he says that she's more
sensible when she's asleep than when she's
awake—-reversing all the nat'ral laws as I'm
acquainted with—then what I says is, I'm
not goin' to be surprised if the schooner's
luck's gone out of her and the worst ye can
fear a-followin' of us in that steamer."

"I tell yer," said Joe Hall, "that the lady
came up asleep. She stared at nothen, past
me till I slipped t'other side the tiller in a
sweat. Then she sensibly talks to the
parson and Mr. Stone at the lee rail, points
and chucks her arms about, asleep all the
time, and goes below missing nothing,
steppin' out true as a hair."

"There's nothing wonderful in that," said
Archer, who had been listening quietly.
"Providence looks after sleep-walkers. I've
heard of women getting on to the tops of
roofs of houses and strolling about on ledges
so tall and narrow that people watching them
have turned sick."

"Well, I only wish the lady was more natural, more 'cording to regulations," said the cook, directing his pale face, full of uneasy workings, towards the steamer. " I never was shipmates with anyone as walked in his sleep afore, and though Providence, as Archer says, may keep a h'eye on the movements of a party given to insensibly h'acting arter the manner of ghosts, my notion is that the sperrit what works in a party and h'enables him or her to conwerse all the way from here with a man suppoged to be in England but 'longside her all the time, can't belong to the part people looks up to when they prays !"

"Why not?" demanded Archer.

"Why not?" echoed the cook. " 'Cause if it was the sort o' sperrit a man has no call to be alarmed at, it 'ud make a party act arter the manner the party was intended to."

"I agree with Micky," observed Goldsmith. " I recollect of hearing a preacher chap at a Bethel say that when the ancient Jews saw a man acting unnatural they calculated the devil had stowed himself away inside of him. How they got him out o' the man I forgets ; but anyhow that notion of the ancient Jews—who weren't bloomin' fools, neither, spite o' Bill grinnin'——."

" I'm a-grinnin'," exclaimed Breeches, " because ye're a-makin' out that that notion you've spoken about belonged to the Jews. Why, man, when I was a lad the idea was common in the willage I was born in. I've helped to duck two old women myself 'cause the belief was they'd shoved evil spirits into folks, and prevented hens from laying eggs !"

This observation led to a lively argument between the cook, Breeches, and Goldsmith as to whether the belief that people who acted erratically, like sleep-walkers, or demoniacally, like Breeches' two old women, were possessed by demons, originated with the ancient Jews or with Bill's village contemporaries.

But the pursuit ! What did that steamer, there, signify ? She was yet hull down, but with all her canvas showing, settling away on the lee quarter ; though now, when Hiram brought his eye from the glass, he informed Stone that she was heading exactly their own course.

" There is no doubt she is after us ?" said the curate.

" Not a shadder of doubt, Mr. Fortescue."

" And she is overtaking us !"

" That's plain, too, sir."

"Suppose she should prove an English-man, captain ?"

" I don't want to find out, Mr. Fortescue. I don't want to have nothen to say to her. As I have told ye, if she ain't a friend it'll be too late when the fact's discovered. Bill, shall we bring the schooner close ? We're being picked up, mate !"

" It won't do to jam her," answered Stone ; "but it might be worth findin' out if th' Hope won't lie closer than t'other can. Half a point——"

" Then down with that stunsail, Bill !" burst out Hiram ; and in a moment old Stone was running forward and singing out. The men, rendered active as cats by anxiety, in a very few minutes had hauled down the stunsail, braced the yards sharp up, and " sweated," as they say at sea, every sheet to a pancake-flatness of canvas. The vessel was kept a rapfull, but the shift of helm

had brought the sea well on the bow, and
the pressure aloft was exceedingly heavy, for
the Golden Hope, sweeping into the breeze,
put a true stormy spite into its hard pouring,
and she drove along like a locomotive, the
spray breaking in snow-storms over her
head, her lee rail pretty nearly flush with
the smother there, her weather standing
rigging like bars of steel for the wind to
split on and rave through, every foreround
of her canvas flashing with a starry light
and melting into pallid dimness with the
reel and stagger of the spars to the sun,
and his dazzling leapings from one cloud-edge
to another. Phew! 'Twas noble sailing, the
flight rather of some beautiful creature of
instinct, maddened by a far-off bellowing in
her wake, than the mechanic movements of
a piece of man's handiwork urged by the
winds and guided by the helm.

The crew gathered aft for the shelter of
the quarter-deck from the tempestuous raining of green water forward, and stood
grouped near the main rigging, all staring, as
with one pair of eyes, at the steamer.
Hiram, kneeling on those legs of his, which

in their trousers looked rather less supple
than a pair of sugar-tongs, inspected the
stranger through the telescope. He watched
her for a long minute, the glass lifting and
falling with his head to the plunge and dip of
the schooner. Then rising and casting his
protruding eyes in the most dismal manner,
first on Mr. Fortescue, then on Stone, and
finally on the men, he said in a low but
hollow voice, " Lads, he's hauled his wind !"

" Headin' up as we do?" shouted Breeches.

" Ay," answered Hiram, " as we do."

" Then," growled Goldsmith, with a note
of desperation in his deep-sea bass, " it's h,
a, double h'ell—h'all, u, p—h'up, h'all h'up,
bullies. What's a-goin' to withstand h'engines
in a wessel as can sail as close as the chase ?"

Hiram took no notice of this.

" But, men," cried out Mr. Fortescue,
" after all, our ideas are pure imagination
so far. How do we know that she is not
an Englishman ? Presuming her to be a
foreigner, what right have we, as yet, to
suppose that the country she belongs to is at
war with us ?"

" Ay, that's all very well, sir," bawled the

cook ; " but what's Captain Weeks running
away for, then ?"

" Because," roared Hiram, "it's one of
them businesses which, to make sure of,
allows 'em chiefly to make sure of *you*.
What's she a-chasing of us for ?   D'ye think
she'd shift her course if she only wanted to
speak—if there was nothen particular?   She's
a man-o'-war, and what's her purpose in these
here waters ?   Why, yes," he shouted scorn-
fully, "she *may* be a countryman, and she
may be mistaken of our dodgin' her.   But
d'ye wish me to heave-to to find out, when
by gettin' away we shall be dropping all the
risks I've told yer about ?"

" But we aren't goin' to get away !" cried
Breeches.   "Why, she's swellin' up, down
there, like a sailor's westkit in a public-
house!"

"She's got a colour flying," said Stone,
who had been silently working away with
the glass.

" Ha !" exclaimed Hiram, wheeling round.

" At the foreroyal masthead," continued
the mate.   He looked a little while longer.
" I dunno," he cried, " my sight ain't what

it was ; but—but if it ain't blue an' white
and red you may bile me," he roared out,
"or if it's yaller, or black, or green?"

Hiram looked on, dully, an instant or
two, staring at Stone. "By thunder!" he
muttered, then snatched at the glass and
levelled it. "French!" he yelled. "Who's
got eyes here?"

The men came in a rush all around him.
Hiram gave the telescope to Archer, who,
after a short inspection, said, "Yes, sir, the
tricolour. A small French screw man-of-
war."

Others of the men looked—Breeches,
Goldsmith, Duck; they were all agreed.
The flag in the glass blew out its tints
brilliant to the sun, and the vessel herself,
her hull now and again showing betwixt a
sea, black and glossy as the plumes of a
raven, was heading up to it like the schooner
herself, and gaining steadily with every five
minutes that went by.

Hiram, folding his arms, took a long look
at the stranger and then a long look at the
men. He was lost in thought ; then awoke
to earnestly inspect his canvas, and judge his

speed by watching the passage of the white water.

"Bill," he said, addressing Stone in a voice to be heard by all hands, "she's catching us up, but we'll keep on this ratch and hold on all, for we're not to know she wants us to stop, and something might happen to her h'engines, or she might carry away a mast—and anyways we'll hold on all!"

Stone nodded.

"But whether there's war or not," continued Hiram, making his eyes meet with a singular look in Mr. Fortescue's face, "that's no call for us, whether we're overhauled or whether we succeed in gettin' away, to feel ashamed of the colours we sail under. So, Bill, out with the h'ensign and run him up."

This was done, and as old Stone hauled the glorious bit of bunting, streaming like a flame as it soared rattling in a graceful curve, to the halliard-block at the peak, one saw the English spirit, acting like the touch of nature that makes the whole world kin, in every man's face, as the whole mob of them followed with their gaze the flight of the meteor flag to its destination at the lofty gaff-end.

"They've hauled down the flag at the masthead," shouted Stone, with his eye at the glass. "Hillo! One—tew—three—four —five flags; they're a-signalising of us; and —hillo!" he bawled again, "they're a-firing!"

The small white ball of smoke, that as it leapt from some bow gun or other of the steamer, was blown by the wind into a stretch of veil-like vapour, was instantly seen, and all hands stared for the missile.

"Well, I'm doodled!" bawled old Breeches. "That's meant for our ensign, I s'pose, an' if it don't sinnify war, why, then, any man may chuck old Bill overboard as likes."

"Anybody see where the shot struck?" shouted Hiram, in a quite desperate state of excitement. There was no answer. "Anybody hear the explosion?"

"Oi did," cried Johnny, with his white face conspicuous among the men.

"Beg pardon, cap'n," said Archer, stepping forward, "but if so be, as Mr. Stone says, that steamer's signalising of us, it's likely she's fired her gun to call attention to her flags or as a request to us to heave-to."

"There's no use in her botherin' with

flags," cried Hiram, whose agitation kept him jumping and hopping about as though his nervous system had been suddenly and violently smitten, "cause we've got no book on board and shan't be able to onderstand nothen but h'ensigns. As to her meaning by her gun to ask us to heave-to, why, if I could believe it wasn't shotted—and that she only wanted to speak us——" and here he stopped with his eyes on Fortescue.

"There can be no doubt, I suppose," said the clergyman, "that she is French?"

"I don't know, sir," answered Hiram. "She may be a Roosian. I tell yer, hoisting colours in war time's mere cheatin'."

"Anyway," pursued the clergyman, "she's gaining on us?"

"Hand over fist," answered Stone. "Them there propellers, I've heerd, often do best when the wind's heading, by the grip they get of the water."

"She's certain to overtake us, then?"

Stone shrugged his shoulders, Hiram turned to look at the steamer, the men glanced over the sides or up aloft. The silence was general and mightily expressive.

" I think we ought to heave-to," said Fortescue, mildly.

" The schooner's yours, sir; you're my master; whatever orders you give'll be obeyed," exclaimed Hiram, rounding rapidly on his long legs and speaking with an eagerness and anxiety that made you see he wanted to be quit of his responsibility.

" What do you say, men?" exclaimed Fortescue, addressing them. " You see how the case stands. Our fears may prove imaginary, but in any case she is certain to outrun us, and supposing it conceivable she should be an enemy we are not going to improve our reception at her hands by a long and irritating chase."

" That seems right enough, sir," said Stone.

" If she's bound to overhaul us," growled Breeches, " why then she must."

" Why, yes, of course, if she dew, she dew," cried Goldsmith; " but somethin' may happen, an' I'm for keepin' all on as we're a-goin'. Time enough to heave-to, says I, when she proper fires at us."

" There goes a second gun, anyhow," observed Archer.

It would have made a monkey laugh to see the fellows staring up at the sails and at the sea to observe where and what the ball was going to strike.

"I tell ye what it is, lads," said James Kitt, throwing a savage, fighting look along the schooner's unarmed deck, "for an Englishman to be aimed at by a Parley Voo without his having so much as a squib to retarn the compliment with, is a dispensation as don't suit my book, for one. An' running away from that three-coloured rag's as little to my taste, too. If it was me, I'd down hellum and chance th' odds."

"Well, I'm agreeable," said Breeches.

"Nothen else to be done, as I can see," exclaimed Sawyer.

"All right, down hellum, then!" cried Duck.

"It's your wish, sir?" said Hiram.

"What choice have we?" answered the clergyman, not without anxiety in his voice, as he looked at the steamer.

"In tor'gan'sl!" bawled Hiram. "Back the torps'l! Down staysail and flying-jib. Up main tack! She's been sweated enough."

The men sprang about, those who would have remonstrated smothering up their objections, and presently the schooner was lying without headway upon her, bowing the long, steady rolling sea with a regular rhythmical swing of stem and stern, everything quiet aloft, and the crew looking over the lee rail at the steamer that had reduced canvas down to bare poles, and was heading for the weather quarter of the Golden Hope, flinging the billows aft in spray over her as her screw drove her headlong through them.

About a quarter of an hour after the schooner had been hove-to, the sudden dropping of the wind was like the weather's confirmation of the wisdom of Hiram in bringing his vessel to a stand. It was certain it rendered the men more satisfied with what had been done, more particularly when they noticed, as the steamer grew upon the sea, the superb shapeliness of her hull, her dominant shearing of the lessening surge rising white to each cathead, the rake of spar whose suggestion of speed was accentuated by the swift pouring of smoke from the leaning

funnel, and the inimitable animation of the
naked fabric as expressed in the pulsation of
blueish light in her wet sides, her shining
leaps from brow to brow with the tricolour
streaming at the gaff-end, where it might now
plainly be seen, and, as old Stone could mark
ere long through the glass, the glittering of
uniforms on the bridge.

The breeze had settled south-east again,
with something of the steadiness of the trade-
wind in it, when the Frenchman, as the
steamer was now by all hands agreed to be,
was about half-a-mile distant. His approach
was watched with an anxiety that became a
kind of fever in the more nervous. Hiram
stood with one hand gripping the other blood-
less, Stone with folded arms, Breeches sour
but with the English sailor's doggedness in
his face, Goldsmith with that anticipative leer
which, as a prophetic expression, is good for
whatever may happen ; and so on. Mr.
Fortescue, holding Agatha's hand, thought to
himself, "suppose Hiram is right—that there
is war between England and France, and we
are taken prisoners !" And you could have
guessed what was passing in his mind by the

face he would turn from the steamer to his
love.

On the other hand, the girl asked no
questions. It seemed to him as if her
imperfect grasp of what was happening
restrained her from interrogating him by
the sensitiveness that springs from one's
knowledge of one's ignorance. He would
see her straining her eyes at the coming
vessel, then glancing from his to the faces
of the men, with a contraction as of earnest
thought in her fair brow followed by a side
peep of wistfulness at him, which, whenever
she caught him notice it, she'd endeavour,
in a manner most affecting to him, to charge
with a meaning he knew it did not possess,
by uttering some commonplace as to the
failure of the wind, the deadness of the blue
water, brimming foamless past the bends of
the stationary schooner, and the like.

The steamer ranged alongside to windward within easy speaking distance. Her
engines stopped, she came to a halt, and
lay rolling upon the sea, showing a broad
white deck with every leeward heave, a
few carronades, a long gun in the bows,

and whole masses of seamen, whose pos-
tures, motions, figures, dress, would have
bespoken her origin and character though
she had come along with the red cross at
all three mastheads and the most familiar
ship's name in the English tongue writ
large on each bow.

"Oh, ze schoonaire, eh-hy?" shouted a
man, twinkling in buttons, from the bridge.

"Hallo!" roared Hiram.

"Vere you boun'?"

"H'ingland!" shrieked Hiram.

"Ve veel send a boat!" bawled the little
chap.

"What for, sir?" cried Hiram.

"Ve have a leetel babee heere, an' ve ask
you to take heem."

Hiram looked at Mr. Fortescue with a face
from which all human expression appeared to
have vanished—answering purely to Jack's
illustration, "As long as a wet swab."

"Well, I'm jiggered!" he rapped out,
bringing his open hand smartly against his
leg, "to think we crew of Englishmen
should ha' been running away all mornin'
from—from a little baby!"

CHAPTER V.

A NEW PASSENGER.

A SHOUT of laughter followed Hiram's exclamation. It was like all hands letting out their breath in a cry of relief and delight. Indeed, the incident seemed a thing incredible after the strain of the excitement all morning. Was the request a sincere one? Was it to mask some manœuvre, to catch the schooner unawares? The fancy seized old Breeches' mind, and he whispered it quickly to those nearest him, in a way to put such faces upon them as would have satisfied any man that if there was to be more laughter from the crew there were three or four who would not join in it.

" Well, Mr. Fortescue, and what am I to tell 'em, sir?" said Hiram, addressing the clergyman, after a long pause full of hard breathing and rolling chuckles, during which something resembling the skipper's habitual expression of countenance had slowly filtered into his face.

" A baby?" exclaimed Fortescue. " Surely a most extraordinary request. Do you think it was 'baby,' he said ? Is there anything else like that word in a Frenchman's mouth he could mean ?"

" He said ba-BEE right enough ; ba-BEE. And what's that word going to sinnify if it don't answer to what it sounds like ?" said Hiram, looking at Stone.

" Well, no use botherin' over what's h'intended, for they mean to h'explain it themselves," exclaimed Stone.

As he spoke, a fine ten-oared boat was swung through the davits of the steamer, and with tolerable smartness she was presently heading for the schooner, with oars quickly rising and falling, and a little glittering man sitting aft, conspicuous even at a distance by an enormous moustache. In true English merchant fashion the crew of the Golden Hope leaned over the side, watching the boat, with their chins upon their bare arms, their faces half-sullen, half-inquisitive. In voices rendered gloomy by the hoarseness of their subdued notes, they criticised the dress of the French seamen, their manner of rowing, and other matters, which gratified them as contrasts highly favourable to the marine sons of " Britannia, the pride of the ocean."

" Truth is," muttered Goldsmith, " 'tain't in the nature of Frenchmen to make sailors. They never take to the sea nat'rally—they're forced to it, and when sailors' clothes is give 'em they don't know how to put 'em on. And how d'ye think they're fed ? Why, on soup ! and they has a thin red wine sarved out t'em, and I tell ye what, mates, nothen comes handy to 'em to lay hold of but a musket. They're never comfortable in their minds till they're put to marchin' up and down like soldiers."

The boat drew alongside and hooked on, the gangway was unshipped, steps thrown over, and the French lieutenant came on board. At the sight of Agatha he pulled off his hat with such a flourish as he would have made on one of his boulevards, and though there was tact in his first manner of looking.

he could not conceal his surprise and admiration. In truth, this monsieur might have spent his life in travelling over the world without encountering in any woman the surprising charms, the wild graces Agatha offered to his eyes, with her hair trembling to the wind, and its auburn full of glory when the sun streamed out upon it, her loose apparel that yet revealed the beauty of her shape, her buoyant swayings to the movement of the schooner; nor could he fail to notice in the expression of her face the lack of something Fortescue might have found him a name for, but which would to an extent increase the fascination of her beauty by filling her brilliant yet soft and pensive stare and the troubled gathering of her fair brows with child-like marvelling and an incomparable *naivete*.

"Veech," said the little Frenchman, smiling and glancing round, after another look at the girl over his great moustache, "is ze capitaine?"

"I am, sir," said Hiram, now quite satisfied that there was nothing hostile in this business.

"I beg pardon," said the lieutenant, bowing.

"Your language I speak bad; there is no one here talk French?"

Fortescue turned to Agatha. She used to speak it fluently; it would test her memory, too. But to his first words she coloured deeply and turned her face aside with an air of distress, to cover which Fortescue said quickly, "I am afraid, sir, we shall be unable to converse with you except in our own tongue. But your accent is excellent."

A profound bow and an overwhelming smile repaid this compliment. Breeches, standing amidst the tiptoeing, shoving, consumedly-curious crew, growled out, "Why the blazes don't he say what he wants? Has he brought us to, jest to bow and cut capers *hay-lee-mode* froggee?"

"Messieurs," said the Frenchman, "den I most do my best. Fairst, I veel ask why you ron away?"

"'Cause we didn't like your appearance, sir; didn't onderstand your chasing of us; couldn't see what you might be wantin' in these here waters," said Hiram.

"Ha!" exclaimed the lieutenant, to whom this reply was barely intelligible, in spite of

Hiram's shouting at the top of his voice, after the custom of the English, who evidently believe that the only way of making a foreigner understand is to start with the assumption that he is deaf, "ve did see you airlee dis morn from zee mast," pointing aloft ; "and as you go fast we raise de steam, but you ron away, which we did not like, because we know if we lose you, anodaire we might not find, and we discharge two gon. Our want is dis. We are on an excursion, geographic, exploratif, for ze government of ze French nation, and we sall be long among de islands here and odaire places. Now, messieurs, it is four days pass dat we meet wid a boat and in it a spectacle distressing ; two dead men and von dead woman, and a leetel babee dat was alive. We keep de babee and ze odaires we sink in de sea. I cannot tell ze nation dey belong to. Name dere was none on ze boat, no tings in dere pockets, no papaire ; von knife, a—vot you call dat ze door open wid ?"

" Key," said Fortescue.

" Yes, key, a vatch, dat is all. Dese tings ve hov. Vell, vot ve do wid dis leetel babee?

Ve hov no voman—no laday. All are men.
But dat, messieurs, is not all. If presently
ve should be going to some port, den ve
might keep de babee; but ve are here for
veek and veek; possib ve might not see a
sheep for day and day; dis vos our imagination ven ve sight you and so ve give ze
chase; ve vould have de leetel babee taken
avay by some sheep dat is sailing to port.
Veel you take it? Ze laday veel not refuse,"
and as he said this again, to the amusement
of the crew, the French lieutenant pulled off
his hat and gave Agatha a bow, perhaps
accompanying it with a leer; for what
Frenchman can resist the impulses of his
profound self-belief in his killing graces?

"A rum yarn, sir," said Hiram to Fortescue.

"I see their difficulty," answered the
clergyman. "They will spend weeks in
cruising about these seas and in parts
where they are not likely to fall in with
ships. I think we should relieve them
of their care; and the little waif may die
in their hands—only what sort of nursing
can *we* give it?" His eye wandered to

Agatha, who was looking at the steamer, whilst the Frenchman stroked the spikes of his moustache, his arm across his breast, examining the girl through his eyelashes with his face bowed.

"I'm not a man to object to babies myself," said Stone, "but seein' that ye've got a h'obligation big enough for two armfulls standin' close beside ye, sir," he looked at Agatha, "I'd consider well, if I was you, afore burdenin' myself with the charge of a h'infant."

"There's nothen onlucky, I suppose, in comin' across a baby at sea?" said Hiram, doubtfully and interrogatively, and in a loud voice so that he might be heard by the men.

Breeches would have been glad to answer this, but as he was unable to recollect any superstition under the particular head of babies, he contented himself with looking as if his mind held several dark recollections but that he would rather not mention them.

"How old is the child, sir?" asked Fortescue of the lieutenant.

" About fifteen munt, monsieur."

" Girl or boy ?"

" Leetel boy."

The clergyman fell into deep thought.
Nothing could ever happen but that he would
accept it as an expression of God's meaning
with him which, whether intelligible or not,
was to be thought of in reference only to his
Maker's love and mercy. What wonderful
purpose lay in this strange encountering of a
tiny bairn in the mighty heart of the ocean?
He felt a superstition come into him out of
the thing. It was not so much that his heart
was moved by the thought of the helplessness
and littleness of the motherless creature
plucked from the edge of a sea grave, as that
he was influenced by some monitory motion
of his spirit urging him to quick decision, as
though there were in him a vision deeper
than his own soul knew of, that saw beyond
what had come and was rendering instinct
imperious.

" Forgive me for detaining you," he said
to the lieutenant, " I wish first to consult
with this lady."

The Frenchman bowed, and Stone and

Hiram, seeing by the curate's manner that however he decided it would be without reference to them, dropped their eager aspect as of men ready to give an opinion, and settled themselves into a cool posture of waiting, with many glances from the lieutenant to his steamer.

"Agatha, my darling," he said, "do you understand what has passed?"

"Oh, yes."

"If we receive the little baby will you see to it, attend to it, care for it?"

"I should love to do so," she answered, gently, speaking with a singular tenderness in her eyes. "It will find me occupation, and there will be always something to think of. I need that. It is cruel to find nothing to fix the thoughts upon."

"It will give you trouble, Agatha; it is a very young baby — fifteen months old, only."

"Poor darling!"

"It will have to sleep in your cabin; it will require your constant attention."

"It is that I need," she exclaimed, with a tremble in her voice and a look like sorrow in one who is dumb passing over her face.

"Be it so," he exclaimed. "The hand of God is in this," and he paused with a hope or fancy in him that made him tremble as if it were a dim revealment, though in an instant he perceived it was one of those pious impositions the brain deceives the heart with when desire is passionate and ever searching for auguries. He turned to the Frenchman, who continued to stroke his moustache and to furtively study Agatha.

"Sir," said he, "we shall be glad to receive the child."

Another grumbling sort of chuckle rose behind the little Frenchman from the crew as he stooped low with his hat to the deck almost.

"You are ver good, saire," he exclaimed, and running to the side he called out to his boat's crew, "Go, my infants, and fetch *le petit*. I stop here till you return." He may have added something else—perhaps winked or made a knowing grimace behind his moustache—for "his infants," as he called the swarthy, uncouth, untidy boat's crew, shoved off in a violent hurry and pulled away to windward as if rowing for a wager.

Fortescue asked him into the cabin to take wine, but he declined with a very polite face, all the while looking about him with great curiosity, more especially at Agatha, by whom he seemed both bewildered and fascinated.

"You have ver nice leetel sheep here, saire," said he to Fortescue, whom he guessed to be the owner by his having for himself decided about the baby, and approaching him that he might also draw closer to Agatha. "You are takin' your plaisaire in her? And ze lady?"

"The lady was shipwrecked; we searched for and have found her and are conveying her home," answered Fortescue.

"Aha!" cried the lieutenant, with a long breath that whistled through his teeth, "den all explain himself. Dat why you here. My capitaine say, 'What dat leetle sheep do here, hein?' Now I can explain him. Sheepwreck! Ha, Ha! I hope, mam'selle, your sofferin' vas not ver great?" giving her a bow.

It might have been the little creature's

stature, or the vanity and self-assurance expressed in his face, with the ends of his moustache standing out past his cheeks like marlin-spikes—and there was nothing more nautical than that to be found in this vulgar ornamentation of the sailor—or the grins of the men which wrinkled their chocolate skins to every bow or grimace this lieutenant made —indeed, they might have passed for a street mob watching a monkey—that broke in upon Agatha's gravity ; she burst into a laugh, and then nervousness mastering her, she continued to laugh with a note of hysteria in her mirth, blushing for her merriment, too, and with a look of helpless shame, amid the sparkling in her eyes, that did undoubtedly make her face a lovely puzzle to monsieur's surprised and somewhat indignant stare.

"Saire," said he, turning to Fortescue, "I am happee to know by ze layday's amusement dat her sofferin have not been ver great," and with that he folded his arms, after the style of the great Napoleon, and fixed a scowling gaze upon the steamer.

It was not a thing to bother over, and Fortescue was in no mood to relate to this

stranger the story of Agatha's shipwreck
and the mental blow that had befallen her,
which any approach to an apology for her
laughter would have involved.   Perhaps
he wondered that the little lieutenant had
not eyes for the truth ; but a life spent in
the cure of village souls must necessarily
leave a man's theory of human conceit imperfect, spite of neighbouring squires and
here and there a parson's wife.   Hiram,
however, on the other hand, grew nervous.

" Bill," he muttered to old Stone, " 'twon't
do to let the little chap sulk.   Suppose when
he goes back he should tell 'em he's been
insulted.   Them there Frenchies are like
what they make grog of—spirits o' wine.
Fire 'em, and they're alight all over !"   So
saying, he convulsed his gaunt and yellow
face into a smile, and stepped up to the
Frenchman.   " Beg pardon, mounseer ; that
there's a fine craft o' yours, sir."

" Varee."

" Long from home, sir ?"

" Four munt."

" Ah, then you'll have no more noos than
we have.   Fine country yours, sir.   I knows

B'long and I knows Cally, an' I was once ashore off Cape Levi and pretty nigh drownded."

The Frenchman said, "Hum," not understanding ; then, screwing up his eyes at Hiram, he said, "You are capitaine, eh ?"

"Yes, sir."

"Ees it true dat lady dere was sheep-wreck ?"

Hiram nodded.

"Anglish ?"

Hiram nodded again.

"Vy she laugh at me?" inquired the Frenchman, rearing his little figure whilst he looked up into Hiram's face, in a manner to remind one of the sketch of the cock threatening to spring at the horse for having tossed his nosebag.

"Why," said Hiram in a whisper, "she ain't quite right in her mind—she's lost what they calls a faculty," and he grinned, in sympathy with the start the little Frenchman gave, and the look of relieved conceit that softened down his scowl.

"Ha!" exclaimed the lieutenant, "I am glad. For me," smiting his little bosom with

his little fist, " I do not like ze ridicule," and
that he had forgiven Agatha on the spot it
was easy for Hiram to see by the ogling and
leering glance the manikin levelled at her.
Weeks wanted nothing better. His apprehension of the little Frenchman's resentment
faded, and with it his fear of the conse-
quences which he had gone so far as to
suppose might take the shape of a parting
cannon-ball when the schooners shifted their
helm for their separate courses, and a started
butt such as had sent old Stone's snow to the
bottom, and which might force them into
some barbarous port with all hands half dead
with pumping. It would be suspected that
Hiram was imaginative; in reality he was
only practical; very anxious to get home,
and oppressed with the old maritime conviction that all foreigners are cowards at sea
and capable of the lowest meanness.

It was past one. The breeze was blowing
radiant and warm, for the masses of vapour
had thinned with the shift. They travelled
in pearl-coloured tufts along the path of the
gentle and humming trade. The sun burnt
steadily with a power in his mirroring that

seemed to heap the water up in flashing, silver, liquid, shining ore, weltering to its own ardent throbbing. All this while the boat remained alongside the steamer, rising and falling just astern of some gangway-steps that had been dropped over the side, and the little lieutenant had broken with impatience from the further soothing speech Hiram had begun, and had taken one or two turns with arms tightly folded and his shoulders nearly up to his ears, when he suddenly exclaimed, "*Enfin!*" As he spoke, a man was seen ascending the ladder against the schooner's side with a little bundle in his arms. The bowman pulled the boat to the steps, and the man entered.

"Here he is, sir," exclaimed Stone to Fortescue, "smaller in quantity than a sailor's shirt rolled up in a handkerchief, and yet with such brains in him may be that whose a-goin' to say the day mayn't come when he'll be able to take a line-o'-battle ship into action, and get a pillar put up for him with his name writ on the foot of it? I dunno how it is, I'm sure, but I never yet could look at a baby without some-

how feelin' that he knowed more than I do,
and that if he could speak, the first thing
he'd say 'ud be, 'Why, Stone, you old fool!
Bin a-livin' all these years and not know
more than what ye've got in yer head?
Git out! Here am I, fresh, niver to my
knowledge was in a church in my life, and
yet I could tell ye more about where ye're
bound to and where ye comes from than
ye'd be able to find out if you was to tarn
to and think for three bloomin' centuries.'
No want of respect for religion in them
there ideas, I hope, sir?"

"No, Mr. Stone," answered Fortescue,
gently, "we must all be as little children,
you know, before we can enter the port
that we are sailing for."

Stone looked gratified. Hiram said, "It's
not everything as Bill says that's to my taste,
but I like his notion of a baby knowing
more'n a man. Pity the like of them notions
aren't more discoursed about at meetings,
'stead of always sendin' the plate round, an'
the parson readin' and pretendin' as if he
wasn't thinking of what folks was puttin' in.
It's all very well for people to say as a man's

heart lies in his purse, and that the way to
test a feller is to see what he'll give, but my
idea is that if a man had nothen in his purse
but his heart he wouldn't be troubled. Now
then, lads, look out for the boat. Stand by
with a line in case that it's wanted."

The Frenchman strutted to the gangway
and was followed by Fortescue and Agatha,
Weeks and Stone. The men clambered on
to the rail to see. Never did a baby excite
more curiosity. Old Breeches had hinted
that in all probability the infant wouldn't
prove natural. " Stand by, bullies ! See if it
ain't of a piece with the rest o' this woyage ;
sorter spiritooal, for that's the word we've
been taught. 'Sides, boys, 'tain't wholesome
for a job like this to come through Crappoos.
They h'ain't got Englishmen's domestic feelings, and if I'd bin the parson I'd ha' left the
young 'un on their hands with the chance of
its h'educating the ship's company in moral
feelin's ready agin they gits home."

A bearded French man-of-warsman, a half-
caste, smiling absurdly, with sidelong half-
ashamed peeps out of the corners of his eyes
at the row of British grinning visages decor-

ating the schooner's bulwarks like the orna-
ments on an area-rail, stepped on board,
holding the baby with the sprawling posture
of hand and arm peculiar in seamen when
labouring under a sense of their awkwardness.

The little creature was a fair-haired baby
boy of about the age the French lieutenant
had named. It would indeed be difficult
to determine a nationality for an infant so
young, but if he were not English you would
have known at all events his parents did
not "belong" to regions to the south of
the English Channel parallels. English he
looked, nor could you have said there was
anything of Denmark or Norway or Sweden
in the pretty tiny face; whilst as to his being
German, why, as Hiram afterwards said,
"His ugliness would ha' been the same as
sayin' 'yaw' to ye; yer couldn't ha' bin
mistook." It was a most perfect baby face,
certainly, thin indeed and pale, dark blue
eyes, and amber-coloured hair curling prettily
under a little red cap. He had been crying,
tears still sparkled on his cheeks, but the
change from the boat to the deck of the
schooner arrested his grief or alarm; he sat

up in the sailor's arms, gazing about him with his under-lip sucked in and his breath shortened ready for further tears, till the sight of old Breeches and the others, staring, frightened him; he made one of those lamentable faces of drawn-down mouths and eyes full of misery with which babies are wont to preface their fits of weeping; but just at that moment, catching sight of Agatha, he cried out "Mamma! mamma!" extending his hands towards her, with a leaping forward that came pretty near to tossing him out of the seaman's arms, and roaring at the top of his little pipes. The girl instantly took him. One saw the marvellous maternal instinct in the yearning, soothing manner of her as she kissed him and held him to her bosom. The touch of a woman's hand, the heave of a woman's breast, the warmth and softness of a woman's lips, were as magic; the baby instantly ceased crying and lay still and comforted in her arms, intently staring with his blue eyes afloat with tears at the sweet and gentle and blushing face that overhung him.

Fortescue turned aside a moment with a

quick lifting of his glance to God. The heart
prays swiftly, and in a breath a man can send
a long wordless message of hope and faith to
heaven.   The French lieutenant was moved.

"It is ver pretty," said he.   "Mam'selle
be ze *maman* to perfection."

She raised her eyes from the baby's face
to his with a smile which, finding no derision
in it, he possibly accepted as a tribute to his
manly appearance, for he instantly looked
happy, and one listened to hear him hum
some gay tune.

"Have ye brought the things the orficer
spoke of as havin' been found in the pockets
of the dead people in the boat," said Hiram
to the half-caste.

The fellow shook his head and showed his
teeth with what Breeches called a "no com-
preney" shrug of the shoulders. The lieutenant, understanding the question, spoke to
the man in French, who at once pulled out
of his shirt a knife, an old silver watch
with a water-discoloured riband attached, a
couple of keys and a short black clay tobacco
pipe.

"Dat is all, messieurs," said the lieutenant.

"Was there nothen in writing—no letters—nothen in the clothes worn with a name on it?" cried Hiram.

"Nottings. Ze bodees was half-dressed—ze escape most have been on ze instant; ve look vell for a name, for any sign, but——" and up went the Frenchman's shoulders. Then with a glance at the steamer he said, "Dere is nottings more, messieurs, I tink. In ze name of my capitaine, shenelmen, I tank you for takin' ze leetel babee." And bowing low, first to Agatha, then to Mr. Fortescue, and then to Hiram, the lieutenant nimbly went to the gangway, and, followed by the half-caste, dropped over the side, evidently delighted with the successful result of his mission, and burning for the ardent felicitations he would receive from his shipmates in the steamer.

"Round with that torps'l-yard, lads," bawled Hiram. "Down main tack. Set the flying-jib. 'Loft, one o' ye, and loose the tor'-gallan's'l. Bill, she'll take all you can give her. This here parley-vooing must be made up for, so you can set stunsails and keep her head off for the Cape o' Good Hope."

And he turned to look at the baby who was sitting erect on Agatha's knee, and who, with wide-open, intensely earnest eyes fixed on the golden tresses its little fists had grasped, was tugging at Agatha's hair, whilst Mr. Fortescue overhung the bairn with an expression of deep compassion in his face.

CHAPTER VI.

THE BABY IS FED.

THERE is a mysterious power in the deep that gives to the meanest thing it tosses upon its vast unquiet breast an interest and solemnity it would be impossible to find in the same degree in objects of high significance ashore. A broken oar, a piece of black, weed-covered timber, a bit of board with a letter or two left upon it, will win the eye and fire the fancy as it passes by, whirling smooth into the ship's wake, or coming and going amid the yeasty folds of the leaping surges ; not more because it may be a hint of disaster, the sordid memorial of great human despair, than because the spirit of the huge solitude, the immense desolation, the immeasurable length and breadth of the ocean is in it, like a quickening by nature of things which grow on land ; so that all that she has of solemnity, of secrecy, of austere mockery the sea gives to man's most unimportant relics ; using them to another disdainful purpose yet, that is, of making them contrasts for her mightiness.

This, to its highest, wildest, most startling extent, is felt by the seafarer when the ocean yields up a living human being out of her deepest solitude. The baby, seated on Agatha's lap, was scarcely to be thought of but in the most prosaic literal light, as an ocean waif that had been snatched from death and was now to be nursed and cared for, whilst the French lieutenant was grinning and flourishing near him and whilst there was a background of hairy, weather-coloured faces to put coarseness and realness into thought, with the slow movements of their jaws upon the concealed quids, and the sour, or sympathetic, or wondering, or indifferent staring of their eyes. But the scene had changed ; the crew were running about making sail ; the schooner had started afresh, and with leaning stem was floating with a long-drawn, gushing sweeping of her whole hull from surge to surge, whitening each hollow as it drew up from under her keel, to the blue sparkles to starboard where the sunshine lay in a glorious throbbing. Already the steamer had hoisted her boat and was breaking aloft into expanses of softly shining cloths with a mere expiring filtering of blue smoke from her raking funnel as, obedient to the impulse of her canvas, she slided round with her head to the north-east, stun-sails fluttering to the weather yard-arms and the tricolour dipping a grateful farewell, which old Stone answered with a like salutation.

Now, the solitariness of the tiny human soul, all that had come into the babe out of the magic within the amusive and deceptive girdle of the waters, could be felt, pitied, wondered at, and that the deeper impulses it furnished were not appreciable only by such a mind as Fortescue's, you would have known by looking at Hiram and marking a tenderness in his protruding eyes that gave a comeliness to his long, gaunt, yellow visage, such as will often come to down-right ugliness when thought is eloquent and pure.

"If it ain't the watch, Mr. Fortescue,"

said he, " I dunno, I'm sure, what else there
is among the h'articles found on the bodies to
h'identify this poor little chap when we gits
him ashore ; in which case life'll be as this
here ocean's bin to him—a big loneliness."

" Poor innocent!" exclaimed Fortescue,
stroking the little fellow's cheek.   " Old
Ocean's caprices are strange.   The rage
that wrecks a stout ship and destroys the
lives in her, spares this morsel of fragility!"

" Ay, sir," said Hiram, "just as I've seen
a butterfly safe and sound in the calm heart
of a rewolving tempest.   What fine eyes
he has ! And don't he show the h'evil pro-
pensities of a miser by keepin' hold with
both fisties of the gold a-streamin' from the
lady's head ?"

Agatha laughed and kissed the child.
"He is a real darling," she exclaimed.   "I
shall make him some pretty frocks, and then
he will look beautiful.   See, Mr. Fortescue,
how oddly those Frenchmen have dressed
him ! This strange thing on his head must
be the top part of a man's nightcap, and
they divided a mitten and stitched the sides
together to serve as a pair of socks.   Oh!"

she added, with a sweet smile, and causing
the little creature to chuckle with the fat
notes of a pleased baby by starting him
on a ride with a movement of her knee,
"what is your name? And as you cannot
tell us, what shall we call you? Malcolm
Hope? That will be taking one name
from you, Mr. Fortescue, and one from your
schooner."

"Yes—Malcolm Hope—nothing could be
better—for the present at all events," said the
clergyman, smiling at her light laugh, but
deeply moved by her animation.

It was a liveliness full of womanly tenderness, with a touch of archness that might have
sprung from her child-like simplicity of delight
in the toy that had been given her; but such
as it was, rendered fascinating by her beauty,
her wild, island, careless manner, it was not
the gaiety of the Agatha of Wyloe. It smote
him with a sense of insincerity; it affected
him as a piece of acting; yet, God knows,
the poor fellow was sensible it was real
enough, and seemingly artificial only because
her impaired mind qualified the spirituality
that made all that she formerly thought,

said, and did, rich with sensibility, lovely and lovable with delightful emotion.

Hiram whispered in his ear, whilst with his eye he feigned to direct the clergyman's attention to the French steamer, " Mr. Fortescue, considerin' she don't know ye an' can't recall the past, it's too wonderful that she should be able to tell us that the gear on the child's head's half a man's nightcap and the socks a split mit—too wonderful, I says, not to be took notice of. I beg your mind to it, sir, askin' your pardon."

The clergyman responded by inclining his head. Here the baby let go Agatha's hair and began to cry.

" He may be hungry," said Fortescue.

The girl looked blankly and with a frightened face at the curate.

" Oh, my poor memory!" she cried. " I never thought he would want to eat ; what are we to give him ?" And now it was to be seen how absolutely recollection was at fault. The picture at that instant was one to dwell upon the mind; baby crying, tears showering down his cheeks, inimitable misery expressed in the corners of his mouth, his blue eyes shining through their sorrow like violets in crystal, and Agatha glancing from him to Fortescue and Weeks in a dramatic posture of wild anxiety, a ceaseless, sheeny trembling down her hair from the blowing of the wind, and her colour dimming to the distress that was quivering in her lip till you looked for a tear in the pure softness of her eyes. Under a high and square press of canvas the schooner was snoring through the water like a wounded dolphin chased by its mates, shadows swung along the decks with every yearning reel from and to the sun, and the cloths on gaff and yard, flashed up by the luminary, had a whiteness that made the fleece of the clouds dingy as they sailed by overhead, along a blue that the noon-tide splendour rendered argentine from where the sun shone to the sea-line, undulating away on the quarter where, like a waning star on the north-east horizon, was the lessening lustre of the Frenchman's canvas.

"What do babies eat?" said Hiram, looking anxious. Stone came up as he said this.

"Why, milk is what is chiefly given to

them, at this child's age, I believe; but we have no milk," said Fortescue.

"Got fowls, but ne'er a cow," exclaimed Hiram, rubbing one eye hard with a knuckle. "Little boy got any teeth, miss?"

"Yes, a few," answered Agatha.

"Why, then," said Hiram, cheering up, "he ought to be able to eat what we dew— not so much of course, but the same wittles. He can't hurt. I remember a man as had had thirteen youngsters by two wives, an expirrience stretchin' over, well, I dessay it wouldn't be fur short of twenty-five year, a-tellin' me that he always gave his little 'uns meat when their teeth came. 'Twas nature's way, he told me, of hintin' when they was ripe for meat and could give up sops."

Fortescue shook his head. Meanwhile, the baby had silenced himself by filling his mouth with the fingers of his left hand.

"Babies has two sets of teeth," said Stone; "these here'll be the first lot, I allow."

"The first lot, of course," answered Fortescue, who knew that, but who nevertheless felt exceedingly stupid and troubled.

"Then meat ain't intended by nature for

h'infants' stomachs till the second lot o' teeth come," said Stone.

"What!" cried Hiram, "d'ye mean to say babies has two sets o' teeth?"

"Yes—sartinly, one arter the other," exclaimed Stone.

"Well, jiggered if h'ever I knew that afore," exclaimed Hiram, and he drove his hands into his pockets with an air that made one see he understood he was an ignorant man and meant to give no more advice.

"Tell ye how I should feed him, miss," exclaimed old Stone, meeting Agatha's eyes, "tarn to an' powder up some white cabin biscuit and make a kind o' gruel or pap of it with warm water. That'll stay his young stomach. Afterwards I'd have a fowl biled, and give him the gravy with a little o' the meat cut up fine. He'll fill out at that, ma'am. He'll be wanting a new westkit every day."

Stone's face was a study as he thus spoke. There was the sailor's half-shyness in him, with the grave earnestness of the simple, literal mind when perfectly serious. Hiram listened with an air of respect; it was clear he was impressed by Bill's knowledge of babies and what was good for them to eat.

"Mr. Stone's suggestions are capital," exclaimed Mr. Fortescue, much relieved; and the baby beginning to make faces again and cry out in squally bursts of wailing, through finding that there was nothing in his fingers to appease his appetite, Agatha carried him below to the cabin where Fortescue, watched by Stone, made a mess of sweet biscuit and water in a cup. The little chap's hunger was great; he seized the spoon with his teeth and wrestled and wrangled with it as though he would swallow it. Stone, with a large grin of sympathy, watched the operation of feeding him with critical attention, but Agatha plied the spoon so dexterously that he only once had occasion to suggest that "a little slower, miss, 'ud be better, as these here h'infants are pretty nigh almost fuller o' wind than they knows how to support; an' your yieldin' to the hurry they're mostly in, when hungry, is bound to aggravate their tryin' complaint—an' tryin' it must be, Mr. Fortescue, as anyone can tell by watching how

they shuts up their legs like telescopes when
the spasms seizes 'em."

Almost immediately after he had been fed
the baby fell fast asleep. His head dropped
back on Agatha's arm, a beautiful serenity
entered the little face, a faint smile lurked
about the parted lips; but though his slumber
was sound his eyes were not wholly closed,
and the dim gleam of blue behind the long
lashes made the countenance death-like with
its smile and its stillness.

"His poor mother!" sighed Fortescue,
gently, with an upward glance.

"Ay, sir," said Stone, folding his arms
and looking down at the child, "God allows
a man but one mother in this world. 'Tis
hard he should ever make her suffer. Better
she should go whilst he's what that baby is,
for then she leaves an angel behind her, than
to keep on livin' merely to see horns and a tail
growin' 'stead o' wings. Ah!" said he, with
a deep sigh, "a man's only got one mother,
but he never knows it till she's gone and he
looks back and reck'lects how he sarved her."

He rubbed his nose and seemed oppressed
with memory. Perhaps he was thinking of

the time when he ran away to sea, more to vex his mother who opposed his wish than because he liked the life, and came home a few months after to find her in the church-yard.

A baby is a plaything you need practice to know how to handle. One sees young mothers looking at their first babies with a sort of fear in their delight and worship, as though nothing but the stern necessity to hold and to nurse, could impel them to accept the dreadful risk of touch. Most girls will have these feelings when they get a baby upon their knee, whether it is their own or another's, and you saw a clear alarm enter Agatha's face when the infant fell asleep: she held herself motionless, she scarcely breathed for fear of disturbing the boy. After a few moments she whispered faintly, "Mr. Fortescue, why does not he close his eyes? It looks very unnatural."

Fortescue thought so too, and glanced at Stone, who, supposing he was expected to answer, said : "Nothen onnatural at all, miss. Its a habit of young 'uns to keep their eyelids a-liftin'. The reason is that in a baby h'every thing's a-growin' so rapid nothen'll keep together. That's why they makes faces, and why their toes twitch."

Agatha seemed to accept this view, in her child-like way, and presently, at the suggestion of Fortescue, carried the baby into her cabin and laid him in her bunk. She was exceedingly nervous, handled the child as if he were some vase or fragile ornament of inestimable value and capable of being shivered into twenty thousand atoms by a fall ; yet the sweetness and love in her nature was affectingly visible in her gentleness and tenderness, and when she had placed the little one on her bed and he, after a start and a long sigh, had fallen into deep sleep again, she stood with wet eyes and her hand to her forehead watching him, Fortescue at her side.

" Does your head pain you, Agatha ?"

" No," with a light forced smile, and she let fall her hand.

"What do you see in this baby, my darling, to make you weep ?" he asked, with his love shrinking from the question, whilst his will—his eagerness to test her—forced the inquiry from his lips.

She was silent for some moments, and then said in a low voice, " He is alone."

" Yes, he is alone, in one sense, yet we know not; we cannot be sure. If his parents were those found dead in the boat he is an orphan, and in that way he is alone. But he has a Father in heaven, my beloved ; it is that which makes human loneliness impossible, otherwise the world would be full of lonely people, the lonelier even, some of them, for their very associations of home, of friends !" He met her tearful glance, repressing a bitter sigh.

" His is a loneliness that makes me feel mine," she said. " I know I am alone——."

" No !" he cried.

"I cannot explain !" she continued. "Sometimes a thought comes like a perception, but passes ; it is as though I had been taken by the shoulder and thrust out into the darkness. Oh, it is so ! I am alone. Oh! more, oh ! more alone than he is !" She pointed to the baby and again raised her hand with a wild gesture to her forehead, and held it pressed there.

He grasped her idle hand, and, checking the passion in him till his voice quivered to the restraint, he said, "Agatha, cannot you realise that you are loved? You have memory to recollect what is now said to you, what now befalls you. Reason to yourself thus: Mr. Fortescue, who holds my hand, tells me that we were engaged to be married—still are—that I shall be his wife when we arrive in England—that I loved him dearly, do still dearly love him, though over the mirror of my heart there has come a film that conceals, but does not obliterate, the reflections in it, that he loves me passionately, that, directed by God, he has sought and found me and delivered me from a lamentable fate, a shocking desolation. Reason thus, my own; as Heaven is truth, so are my words. You are following what I am saying—my loved one! Reason thus—reason as I bid you, feel, though you may not fully understand, that you are mine—that you are my Agatha—my betrothed—my only love as I am yours! The thought will soothe you, you will know that you are not alone, and 'twill give you heart and patience to wait with me for the dawn

that must come—for the dawn, my darling,
that must come !"

She had been watching him under the
hand she held to her forehead. When he
ceased she covered her eyes with it and said,
" I will do what you wish. I shall be able to
remember what you say. And I will seek
heart and patience in it."

The icy mechanicalness of this answer,
coming out of sheer incapacity to understand
him as he endeavoured to render himself
understood, so affected him that he dared
not speak lest his voice should break into
inarticulate sobs. He raised her hand to his
lips and let it gently fall, and turned to the
child, concealing his face. These were but
early times, he knew. It was but yesterday
that he had found her ; God alone knew what
might need to go to the vitalising of her
dormant faculty, if indeed it was a slumber
from which an awakening was possible ; but
for all that, it was like to craze his brains to
find his appeals falling dead from her intelligence which they could not penetrate, to see
the life and health and beauty in her and
know that a sudden anguish of terror, like

a wizard with his wand, had banished them
and her heart's love to a sphere outside his
own existence, so far as she had knowledge
of it.   It was as though he should have
wasted his soul in passionate yearnings for
her throughout the voyage, and arriving at
the island at last, have found her enchanted
into stone.   It was bitterer even than that;
for the stone would have been lifeless, it
would not have innocently mocked the sacred
and beautiful devotion of the man by the
lifting of soft grey eyes in whose sweetness
lay no knowledge of him, by speech cruel as
the echo of tones which had been full of his
name and of her love for him, by smiles and
laughter sadder to him than her tears,
though he knew them to flow from the dim,
mysterious sorrow and the vague sense of
loss in her.

He turned presently.   "The little one
sleeps well, Agatha."

"Yes," she answered, with no further
trace of grief in her face than a look of
soberness.

"I hope the care of him may not greatly
tax you.   We must get a kind of cradle or

little bedstead made, so that in the daytime he can sleep on deck, and be close to your hand at night."

"That will be pretty—the little, little fellow! And I will make him clothes. May I take what I need?" with a glance at the large box which contained her apparel.

"Whatever you require. There are plenty of needles and thread. I think you will find all you need."

"Mr. Fortescue, beg pardon, sir," said Hiram, in a hoarse whisper outside, "but dinner's on the table, and it's about time, tew."

CHAPTER VII.

THE BLINDNESS OF THE MIND.

You will often get long spells of glorious weather in the Indian Ocean on the Madagascar parallels and below the tropic of Capricorn to where the trade fails. It is always best of course to be sailing to the southward, for then every day finds a sweeter freshness for the winds and for the atmosphere of the night that follows, and takes out of the sunlight something of that dazzling brassiness of glare that further northwards comes down upon the sickly swell, to steam up off it in a fog-like yellowness of scorching effulgence into which the jibbooms go writhing like snakes whilst the lengths of black yards are tremulous in it, and vapour creeps up from all about with a stink of paint and oil till you are fit to cast yourself into the slimy sea for sheer loathing.

The breeze did wonders for the Golden Hope's latitude. She had such a chance as Hiram would have prayed for. There was steady weight in the wind, a long, light, beam swell that swung her as she ran; all cloths she had she could and did show, and you quitted the deck at night only to witness the same sight next morning—square-sail, topgallant-sail and three stunsails, jibs, staysail, huge mainsail, foresail, and topsails all doing their work, obscuring at night a great expanse of the glittering dust of the heavens with their glooming surfaces, or leaning beautiful, bland, star-like, to the morning azure where spaces of full-bosomed liquid sapphire flowed into lagoons of lighter blue, with wings of pearly vapour steadfastly sailing onwards down the dyes in the airy cerulean acclivity, like ships passing over a sea streaked with tints and melting hue into hue from the movements of currents or the gliding of cloud-shadows.

Life on board had the same sea-going monotony for all excepting Fortescue. Such superstitions as the crew may have felt had gone away over the side into nothingness

along with their tobacco smoke.   Archer had
put them right ; as a fine seaman, who had
nothing professionally to learn from any man
among them, who was as versed in fore and
aft seamanship as he was accomplished in the
more complicated mysteries of the full-rigged
ship, who had held a post of command,
honour, and responsibility on board a great
Indiaman, why, he easily headed all hands,
unknowing that he did so, and whatever he
said about sailorising, and even other matters,
in his careless, sagacious way, was mostly
accepted—even by the cook—as the views of
a man who argued as if he always knew what
he was talking about.   He admitted the
wonderfulness of the clergyman's vision, but
he knew so many cases of verified dreams,
not less remarkable because they were less
elaborate, that through hearing him converse
old Breeches became a convert.

"There must be somethin' in a man's
dreamin', mates," he said, "and I'm a-goin' to
believe in dreams.   Why, see here : suppose
as I should dream that there was a bagfull o'
soverins stowed away in a chimbly easily
found by the pictur' as was put before me in

the wision; what a blooming fool I should think myself arterwards if I was to say, 'No, it's only a dream; there's nothen in a dream,' and I should tell a man what I'd seen in my sleep and he should go, unbeknown to me, and find the money."

In the same way Archer brought the simple-hearted fellows to understand that sleep-walking and the operation of memory in somnambulism were not to be considered as indicating anything ghostly or unnatural in the victims of such habits; and by telling them about Miss Fox's behaviour after the wreck, and explaining to them how, in his opinion, it was that her old beauty came back to her, and more health than she had enjoyed (from all accounts) before leaving England—for it must be said here that when the cook heard that Agatha had sailed in bad health, but that shipwreck made her feel better, and that she ended in becoming wonderfully well on the island, "Jest a place, lads, where ye'd think a rat 'ud pine away," he began to talk of miracles, and to hint that there must be more than something ordinary and proper in a woman who could appear to

a man on the other side of the world in a
dream, and get health and spirits out of
being cast away—I say, by Archer talking to
the men about these things, it ended in the
crew casting adrift their foolish fancies, and
thinking and speaking of the girl they were
carrying home as a young lady who had
undergone a dreadful marine experience, and
had come out of it with faculties stupefied by
suffering.

This sensible view they took pretty easily,
spite of the foreboding head-shaking, and " I
know better" looks of the mule of a cook,
who was the last man to agree to it, and they
were unconsciously helped by Agatha herself,
who seemed to come upon them with another
individuality altogether, when, on the third
afternoon after leaving the island, she arrived
on deck with the baby in her arms, her beautiful shining hair coiled soberly away upon her
head that was crowned with an almost new
straw hat of wide brim, which old Stone, with
a purple blush, had offered her, after passing
a long watch on deck in agitated considera-
tions whether if he named and produced this
hat the act would not be regarded as a piece

of impertinence, though all the while feeling sure that the sealskin cap was tormentingly hot to wear and quite likely by its weight to keep her memory weak.

The hat proved the one thing needful; she received it with delight, and old Stone fell into a posture of transport when, with her sweet smile, she lightly placed it on the auburn tresses her lover had helped her to wind about her head, and turned to the old man for his approval. What imaginable head-gear is there—from the ghastly cave out of which the excellent Sister of Charity peers, to the bonnet that is smaller than a man's hand—which a beautiful face will not lend a witchery to?

"Ah!" said Stone, with a rousing sigh, "I bought that there hat, Mr. Fortescue, in th' highway, off a Jew as asked six shillin' for it and took two. If he was to see it now he'd go an' make his fortune right off by setting up a shop in the West H'end, and sellin' of them hats to the females of the nobility as the most ornamental and h'improving things in that line ever introduced into Europe."

The crew found her attractions strictly within their conceptions of natural things when she presented herself with her hair dressed instead of down her back, where it had rendered her beauty wild in the sight of the mariners, with the long, windy flowings of its shining thicknesses ; and they understood her the better for old Stone's hat; they instantly twigged the nautical cut of it, and accepted it on her as a wide compliment to the profession of the forecastle.

" Nothen unnatural there now, anyway, Mickey," said Goldsmith, with a grin at the cook, who stood with his head out of the caboose, mopping his streaming face and looking aft.

" Well, p'raps not," answered the cook, acidly.

" Tarn to and set her agin upon the h'island, and I dunno, if I was asked, if I'd take a fortnight to make up my mind to jine her."

" Well, I don't s'pose you would," said the cook.

" For, though I'm no longer a young gent, I presarves the feelin's of a man," continued

Goldsmith, smiting his naked breast, "and onlike Bill Breeches, who's got no taste, I'm always admirin' what strikes my nat'ral h'ideas of feymale loveliness as bein' most up to the knocker."

Saying which, he winked upon the cook who, with his gaze stedfastly fixed aft, said, " Well, in that there nautical hat I ain't a goin' to say she's *not* up to the knocker."

She passed her time in making clothes for the baby, in washing, tending, looking after him. She loved the lonesome little creature quickly, and there is no doubt her heart went to him soon, not more because he had a prettiness of face and tricks that accentuated his natural appeal to her maternal instincts as a woman than because his case seemed like hers. He was alone, as she felt herself to be, his brief past of a few months would be a darkness in him that there was no mother's memory to illumine, as hers was a blackness of years, with interests, passions, associations hidden in it never to be disclosed to her, as she often thought when, with her forehead leaning on her hand, she would secretly gaze at Fortescue or follow him about the deck

with eyes hardened out of their softness into
bitter, troubled bewilderment.

Amongst them the men, on hearing that it
was wanted, "knocked up," as they called it,
a very comfortable wooden crib for the baby;
a pillow or two made a good mattress, and
in this contrivance the little fellow slept at
night beside Agatha's bunk, whilst, the
weather keeping very fine, it would be
brought on deck by day for the boy to snooze
in or sit up in and play with the toys some of
the crew made for him.   It was natural that
all hands should soon grow fond of him.
You would see Duck, or Goldsmith, or old
Breeches, after having been relieved at the
helm and walking forward, stop to look at the
little one if he lay sleeping, or to talk to him
if he was awake.   What was best and truest
in these sea-dogs you'd find in their faces at
such times.   The beautiful calmness, the tran-
quillity, with the soft light of a delicate smile
upon it, they saw in the sleeping child was
like a beneficent impulse to them, and it was
a sort of miracle in its way to observe the
habitual sourness of Bill Breeches' expression
melting into a rough, salt tenderness, when

noiselessly and almost breathlessly he would peer at the slumbering boy under the little awning that was stretched over the crib—establishing the most amazing contrast in life by the juxtaposition of his knotted and wrinkled and discoloured countenance, that might have been carved out of a junk of salted horse, with the marble-like features of the baby; or, when finding him awake, he would ask him how he felt and exhibit the most emotional interest in the rude rag doll or much ruder horse, which the child would invite him to admire by frenzied clutchings at, or in the direction of, the objects and by signs and sounds of a character quite untranslatable.

"D'ye know, Hiram," said Stone, "I rather like the way old Bill notices the baby. I fancy if it wasn't that he thought he was bein' watched he'd make more of the h'infant. It's nat'ral. It ain't put on. But who'd ha' supposed it of Bill? To think of him a-takin' to a baby is like conceivin' of an old whale offerin' of its services as a monthly nuss to a young grampus in a h'interesting situation."

"Bill's been knockin' about in all parts for

so many years," rejoined Hiram, "that if it wasn't that there was nothen in the 'spression of his h'eye when he fixes it on the kid to make one fanciful, I might conclude that his likin' for the child was a matter o' conscience."

"As how?" said Stone.

"Well," answered Hiram, "I once knew an old sailor as was noted for his affection for Jews.   This was reckoned so queer that all sorts of guesses was made to get at the reason.   If he was cheated by a Christian he'd fly into a fearful passion, but if a Jew choused him he'd say nothen.   Well, it tarned out that he'd been one of a ship-wrecked crew adrift in a boat along with a H'israelite that was a passenger ; they cast lots and eat up the Jew.   It wur superstition, of course ; but he'd afterwards own he must ha' swallowed some o' the prejudices of that race along with the Hebrew passenger, for though he remained a Methody, which wur his native religion, he never could look a Jew in the face without the feelin's of a brother."

"And you mean to say——" said Stone.

"Well, ye know, Bill's knocked about, and

babies aren't so scarce, but that in thirty or forty year o' seafarin', Breeches may have been shipmates with one."

You do not go to sea for sentiment; yet Hiram, who could not understand softness in the forecastle hand, was always quick himself to yield to the influence of the baby's innocent, flower-like eyes, his smiles, his tears, his beauty in sleep.

" Arter all, sir," he once said to Fortescue, after a long look at the child, and speaking with a half aside at Agatha, "there's a some- thin' wonderful civilising about a baby. I never was married myself, and don't want to, an' have so little acquaintance with babies that there's ne'er a man as could know less about 'em. Yet I can understand, by noticing the sort of homeliness that little chap has brought to the schooner, why parties as marries don't find their home comfortable an' shipshape ontil there's a young un a-singing out in it. 'Tain't only his woice; there's the confugion and mess he brings along with him, clothes a-h'airing, pair of shoes half as big as a man's thumb on one cheer, pair of small socks on another

cheer, flavey o' milk in the air and a smell o'
physic atop of it.   When ye enters a house
where there's a baby ye feel at liberty to
draw out your pipe and smoke, for it's like
bein' at home ; the people are kinder, they
makes more room and 'lowance for a man,
the baby's thawed the frost out, and the
furnicheer looks as if it was used to bein'
sot upon.   But the house where the baby
ain't yet come—well, I'll tell yer, sir, I don't
care how cheap coals is, but all the blazin'
fires married parties can keep up isn't going
to give out one touch of the warmth ye'll get
from an infant's smile—ay," he added, ener-
getically, "even when it's produced by wind."

Having delivered this speech he gazed
first at Agatha, then at Fortescue, and finally
at the baby, with an expression of grave
satisfaction, which was improved into a slow,
but steadily expanding smile by the clergyman's assurance that his sentiments did him
honour.

But meanwhile, though day after day was
passing, the girl made no sign.   Memory remained frozen, black, motionless.   No light
Fortescue flung upon it found reflection.

Often he would essay—faintly, indeed, for there always seemed a cruelty in it to his love —to touch some chord the mere vibration of which should bring intelligent pensiveness, the wistfulness of even dimmest recollection to her face, but unavailingly. The memory he sought stared blankly at him from her eyes; a little pertinacity on his part would cause her to droop her head, to press her brow, to weep silently, and these were things which always broke him down and filled him with bitter self-reproaches.

And yet, as the days passed on, he began to see very clearly that her liking for him increased. She was won by his devotion, by his anxiety. It would be impossible to say decisively of one in her mental condition that though it was mere bewilderment which his references to their being betrothed, to her becoming his wife on their arrival home, to their having been and still being impassioned lovers, excited in her, she was not affected by them as ideas which were meaningless to her in respect of the past, but which she could understand as words and thoughts to the extent of her comprehension this side her memory. Who could pronounce? Figure yourself incapable of recollecting a single circumstance of your life past a given period.   If you were told that such and such were the conditions of your existence, preceding the loss of your memory, you could understand the meaning of the sentences pronounced without finding in them the intelligibility they would possess if you could associate them with, or perceive that they expressed, the facts they represented. There is no question that Agatha understood, on the information of her lover, that she was his betrothed, and was to be his bride.   If bewilderment and curiosity were the sole effect produced in her, so far as these assurances of his respected her blank past, are we to suppose she would not understand his language as referring to him—to the man himself—speaking to her, moving before her, and impressing her existing power of memory by his continual presence, and by the tenderness and sweetness of his bearing?

Well, if we are unable to see what passes

in one another's mind when we are intellectu-
ally sound, we are not very likely to penetrate
the thoughts of people whose spiritual conditions are out of gear by the dropping away
of one of the most essential and vitalising of
human faculties, and in whom inquiry simply
breeds a sense of painful puzzlement. That
she walked no more in her sleep Fortescue
could not possibly tell, because regularly
every night he turned the key in her cabin
door, lest, should the dangerous impulse seize
her, she might steal on deck unheard and fall
overboard She was perfectly aware of his
practice, but asked no questions, showed no
curiosity ; accepting this, as all other things at
his hands, with a child-like, uninquiring ac-
quiescence infinitely touching, because it was
like her owning that she knew her want and
felt she must be counselled and directed.

Yet at other times, when quietly watching
her, his thoughts would take a little light from
hope. It was then he fancied he could see
in the presence of the baby a direct manifest-
tation of God's controling and directing hand,
as he had imagined when the impulse of his
faith determined him to receive the ocean waif.

Once, her cabin door being open whilst she was dressing the child, the day being calm, everything quiet, saving now and again the creak of a timber, the slight jar of the rudder upon its post, he lingered a minute or two, hearing her voice, to catch what she said.

"Baby, you are straight from God—all little ones are. The light of Heaven upon you has not had time to darken. Oh! flash that lustre upon my mind, poor lonely infant! Make me see into the dreadful blackness in which my life is buried! Oh! baby, be an angel to me! God's light is still upon thee! Make me see! Make me see! Oh! give me remembrance!"

The devoted tone of her voice made her words sound like a prayer to the Almighty. It was as though she sought to purify her human pleading by transmitting it to Heaven through a baby's spirit. She sighed with a sobbing sound, and presently continued :—

"What is it that hinders me from remembering, baby? Why is all that went before my awakening on the island as blank to me as the past is to you? Oh! little one, holy as you are, sinless, with God your only father, coming to us from the loneliness of the sea, solitary as an angel lingering awhile upon the earth—hush! the heavenly Creator understands the sounds you make, interprets your smile, for till knowledge of the world comes to you, your thoughts are wholly and purely of the kingdom of your Father, little one! Be as a guardian spirit to me—plead for me—ask for the light that is now denied me!"

She paused abruptly, stooped and kissed the child passionately, and fell again to quietly sobbing, as her lover could tell by the sounds of her respiration.

CHAPTER VIII.

STONE ADVISES.

THE Golden Hope rounded the Cape of Good
Hope to a steady, glorious, pouring gale, a
little to the north of east, and this noble slant
was throughout the little ship considered to be
so unusual that all hands accepted it as a piece
of extraordinary good luck.   Night and day,
night and day, the schooner speeded before
this roaring wind, out of which the vessel's
swiftness took half its weight and spite, though
it was more than she would have dared show
a double-reefed topsail to had she been looking up into it. The crew had never been more
in love with her. They hove the log regularly,
and the return showed from eleven to twelve
knots, with the same punctuality.   Every day
at noon Hiram ogled the sun through his
old sextant, with as many blandishments of
countenance as his elongated face would

have assumed had he been courting his
sweetheart.

And this went on till they were sheer round
the Cape, climbing northwards. Then followed
some baffling weather, but it was hoped the
south-east trades were not far off, and it
would need some days of bothersome airs to
weaken in their hearts the music that had
been stormed into them by the blowing of the
noble easterly gale.

But all this while Agatha made no sign.
The child engrossed her. It might be,
indeed, that she found her own loneliness
subtly and profoundly reflected in the solitariness of the little waif. It might be that
the yearning, maternal instincts of the girl
noted a responsiveness in the bairn, when she
talked to him, as was her wont, and told him
how lonesome she was, and how bitter her
life was made by the darkness upon her mind ;
and that this inexpressible sympathy brought
him so close to her heart, that had she been
his mother, he could have crept but very little
nearer to her love. It is certain that she
never wearied of him, never disclosed the
least sign of impatience when his restlessness

broke her rest at night, or held her to his side
all day. Most of her leisure was devoted to
making clothes for the little creature, in feeding, attending and waiting upon him. That
emotion was not dead in her; that, indeed,
she could love, was proved by her devotion
to the babe; but it was no expression of
such capacity of affection as Fortescue
sought. The problem grew desperately dark
to the poor fellow. He felt he should only
have rescued this girl to restore her to her
friends, and to be hereafter to her as an
acquaintance merely. It was terrible for him
to consider that his dream, his God-guided
passage, the awful and mysterious vindication
of his Maker's ways to him, should terminate
in the practical divorcement of her heart from
his, and in a separation of love, which, on her
side at least, even if they should become man
and wife, could not be completer, so far as
this world was concerned, were they lying
side by side at the bottom of the ocean.

The men forward were scarcely likely to
critically observe what was going on aft, in
respect, at least, of the sentimental features
of the life there. To Jack it was enough that

the parson had found his girl, and was bearing her home. This filled up his mind, and there was no room for any of the romantic points. Archer, it is true, once said to Goldsmith :—

" I'm afraid Mr. Fortescue will have a deal of difficulty with his lady. She don't recollect more, now, of anything that passed before she was shipwrecked than she did when she was on the island. I suppose there's nothing in loss of memory to stop a female from marrying. Yet it must be queer to feel that you've courted a girl, made her presents, kept company with her, taken her to the theayter and spent your money on her, and then when you're married, for her to look at you and not know who you were, afore say two or three months ago."

" Well, I dunno," says Goldsmith. " I've been married myself. She was a nice gal, and I gave her a funeral up to the knocker. But she and me used to have some shindies, I can tell ye, and all because of her memory. She'd recollect parties I'd been courting before, and quarrels me and she had had ; and so accurate was she in her memory that there was only two things as ever I can remember her being wrong in; one was her age, and t'other the money as she'd had out of me. Now, without memory, she and me might have sailed along without ever fouling."

"Ay," says old Breeches, who had been listening to this, and speaking as he brought the sooty bowl of his pipe so close to his nose to peer into it that he squinted horribly, "and there's another good thing in a woman's having no memory, as you're taking no account of, mate; and that is she'd forget she ever had parients. So that there'd be no fear of a man being chased round the table by his mother-in-law, as was a common occurrence in a family circle what I was acquainted with."

Those were the forecastle views of the matter; but Hiram and Stone—more particularly old Stone—by being aft, and living close to Fortescue and Agatha, saw the clergyman's trouble pretty clearly, and felt a sympathy for him in a rough, homely, salt fashion, indeed, yet with good sense. They both considered themselves under a sort of obligation to soothe and encourage him; but unhappily the subject was a delicate one;

more than that, it was a trifle out of their
range.

"After all," Hiram once exclaimed to
Stone, "what's men like me and you to say?
'Tain't as if he was only an ordinary gent;
he's a parson who's bin a-studyin' of the soul
ever since he left college, and as this here
matter of mem'rys h'intillectual, and as whatever's h'intellectual consarns the spirit, what's
you an' me a-goin' to point out to him that he
don't know?"

"True," answered Stone, "I've given the
subject a good deal o' thought, and I've come
to the conclusion that this here's a traverse
th' A'mighty intends the parson should work
out for himself. Still, it's a bad job, it's a
bad job, Hiram. To love a beautiful young
lady like Miss Fox, to save her life by a
miracle that ain't to be beat in Holy Writ,
for her not to know that you loves her,
and for you to onderstand that if ye could
only wipe the mist off the lookin'-glass of
her mind she'd be more yours than ever
she was afore——it's a bad job, I says;
almost proper to drive a man into getting
his head shaved and chuckin' all the

wanities of life out o' the top window of a monasteery."

Yet spite of old Stone's belief that Fortescue's trouble was a thing not to be eased, or even come at, by such as he and Hiram, he had nevertheless one or two ideas in his mind which he fancied might help the clergyman a bit, in the way of hoping, if he could manage to impart them. The chance came. It was a peaceful night with a broad and brilliant shield of moon shining. The schooner was to the south yet of the Polar verge of the trade-wind, though at any hour the clouds of that steady breeze might be showing, with the welcome wind itself flashing full into the drum-like canvas of the Golden Hope. The stars shone in beauty, and the light heaving of the sea, in the direction of the course of the vessel, gently accentuated the propulsion of the air that was blowing over the quarter.

It was ten o'clock. Stone had the watch, and Hiram had turned in. Fortescue came on deck, and began to walk up and down with his hands behind him and his head bent, without eye for the splendour of the

night.   For ten minutes he continued pacing the deck, then crossed over to Stone,
and said, with the abstraction of a man
whose mind is full of the subject he enters
upon :—

"Mr. Stone, do you know if Archer ever
speaks of Miss Fox's memory ?"

"I can't say, sir, I'm sure," answered
Stone.   "The subject's a delicate one, and
as he's a sensible man I don't reckon that
he'd be making it a matter of talk amongst
the crew."

"He was associated with her some time,"
said the clergyman.   "He may have noticed
signs in her when she was the light-hearted,
leaping creature we found her to be on our
landing — signs which may have become
obscure by the change to the life here;
and he may have his opinions.   I do
not care to question him ; I doubt the good
of it.   He would of course desire to cheer
me, and would hesitate therefore to give me
his true view.   I thought perhaps you might
know if he ever talked on the subject freely,
and what he said.   But no matter, Mr.
Stone.   'Tis· a bitter ending to a voyage

begun in hope—so successful, too, as a discovery—and carried on under God's holy
eye! Almost anything but this! *Anything
but this!*"

His voice trembled as if he would give way,
and he turned to the rail with a deep sigh,
and leaned over it, letting his gaze run along
the glittering path of moonlight till it rested
on the bland and serene orb, where it remained fixed for some moments whilst his
lips moved.

"I shouldn't despair, sir," said Stone,
gravely. "If Hiram and me haven't seemed
to take any particular notice of what's going
on, it's bin, as him and me was not long ago
saying, because it's a matter on which men
like us don't feel ourselves competent to
intrude. But for all that, sir, and the Lord's a-
lookin' into my heart as I speak, I don't think
that ever an hour goes by but what I'm
a-thinkin' of ye both."

The clergyman put his hand upon the
back of the other.

"Ye'll forgive me, sir, for bein' candid,"
continued the old seaman, "but my view is
you're allowing this here loss of memory to

prey upon your mind before you've given the thing what I may call a fair chance."

"I should have hoped," said Fortescue, gently, looking at Stone, "that the mere sight of me—of the man she loved, that she was to have been married to—would have proved the greatest of all chances that could have been suggested."

"Why, yes, sir," said Stone, "but since it's failed, there's no use in considerin' of it as a chance."

"But what is to recall her recollection?" exclaimed the clergyman.

"Well, there's no tellin'. In a big complaint of this kind it's often a little thing as makes it well. First of all, sir—and I know ye'll excuse me—what's wanted, to start with, is patience. Patience is hope, and hope carries people to Heaven, don't it? I'll give ye an example of patience. A savage, belonging to an island in the South Seas, came aboard a vessel, and took a fancy to a needle which he saw the sailmaker using. He tried all he knew to get that needle, offering enemies' skulls, mats, cocoa-nut shells, carved out wonderful, and all sorts of things of a like

kind, but the sailmaker wanted the needle,
and wouldn't part with it. So the savage,
seeing a crowbar near the hatch, steals it,
and goes ashore, and tarns to, with the head
of a wooden spear, to smoothe that there bar
into a needle. Five years afterwards the
same wessel touched again at the same
island, and the crew were told that the
savage was still a-scraping away at that
there bar. He hadn't altered its appearance much, but the general 'pinion was he
intended to keep all on till death brought
him up with a round turn. Patience kept
that savage full of hope, and whilst he had
hope, that crowbar was as good as a needle
to the poor fellow."

Saying which, Mr. Stone furtively hooked
a small plug of tobacco out of his cheek, and
gazed at the clergyman with the complacency
of a man who feels that he has produced an
impression.

"But it was not quite that I meant to
mention, sir," he went on, observing Fortescue
to turn his glance languidly to the sea. "You
say that the lady should have known ye, and
she ought to, there's no doubt. But the

sarcumstance not happening proves, as I
afore said, that if you remove yourself, sir,
from this here schooner, what's there formiliar
about the crew and the craft to catch hold of
her recollection? That's the question. She
looks at me, and she looks at Captain Weeks,
and she runs her gaze over the faces of the
crew, and there's nothen as is beknown to
her. Therefore," he exclaimed, putting some
energy into his voice, which he instantly
corrected after a swift glance round at the
man at the tiller, "what I would like to say
is, afore ye abandon the job as a hopeless one,
wait for the chances that land's a-going to
bring. Take that little village of Wyloe. I
was only there once—that time when I went
to see ye, sir—but as much of it as I looked
at I can now recall as plainly as if there was
a painting of it afore me. And why? 'Cause
there ain't too much of it to crowd the
memory."

Fortescue had turned to him and was now
listening. The old sailor noted this, and
went on with emphasis.

"Wait, sir, till she sees the house as she
was accustomed to stop at, till she's been

curtseyed to by folks with formiliar faces, as
knew her and as'll be delighted to see her
again ; till she meets with the ladies and
gents as are her relations and good friends ;
till she sees ye up in the pulpit in the gownd
she was accustomed to observe you in on
Sunday, a-preaching, in the woice she knew,
the same sort of sermons as used to take her
fancy ; with the congregation a-sitting round,
all known to her, and the old church there
just as it was afore she sailed for India.
Why, who's a-going to say even that her eye
mightn't strike upon a h'eepetaph, as words
writ upon tombstones is called—a h'eepetaph
'graved upon a stone in the buryin' ground
she is accustomed to pass through, which
might sarve her as a light from a bull's-eye
flashed upon the darkness of her mind, and
showin' up to the sight of her sperrit everything ye desire her to recollect ? What I
says is, Mr. Fortescue, that ontil ye sur-
rounds her with all the sarcumstances which
is only to be found ashore, ye'll not be giving
her a fair chance ; and therefore ye should
have patience, sir."

A hint from the most plain and unlettered

sense will often put the keenest intelligence
right. A sailor would know that land is not
far off by the sight of a bird or a piece of sea-
weed ; yet he might not have the knowledge
to steer for it. Stone's rough, rude, salt language contained a hint that Fortescue's own
mind might not have given to him. Indeed,
there would be a perfectly natural egotism in
the clergyman to forbid him from seeing out
of his own brains the chance he yearned for,
for Agatha, when she had shown that there
was nothing in him, in his face, in his speech,
in his efforts to touch her recollection, and win
her memory back. His grief and love kept his
eyes fixed in one direction. It was enough
that she had no knowledge of him. He
never thought of casting his fancy around
or beyond that consideration. But when
he quitted Stone and resumed his walk
about the deck, he thought very earnestly
over what the old man had said, and found
so much hope in it that he felt a livelier
spirit rising in him. It was like a sudden
and great opening of the prospect, and of
course he wondered at himself, that he
should need the words of an old sailor to

make him understand how much of the
sorrow and hopelessness which had come
to him lately with Agatha's increased dejec-
tion and gloomier abstraction of manner,
was due to the absolute egotism in his
theories about her. What, he reasoned,
could be more sensible than Stone's advice
to him to throw his individuality, his personality aside, as a thing no longer to be
dealt with in any present consideration of
her darkened mind? It had failed as an
appeal. It was no good. He must hope
for something beyond that now, and the old
sailor had told him what he might base
sound expectations upon.

He paused to realise the thing himself;
and, standing and looking away into the
darkness over the stern, he conjured up a
picture of Wyloe, of the old church, of the
seashore along which he used to wander with
her, hand-in-hand, passing hours in that way;
of the avenue under whose green twilight he
had first spoken his love, and where, after she
had sailed in the Verulam, he had stood with
folded arms leaning against a tree, with the
tide of moonlight gushing full upon him,

thinking of her. He pictured these things
and his heart took a higher pulsation to the
thought that surely, surely in such a crowd
of gentle, peaceful and beautiful associations.
as that little village of Wyloe would offer,
there must be a magic to touch her memory,.
to brighten out the dreadful darkness into
full knowledge, and give her back to him as
she was in the days of her love and of her
undimmed faculties, the sweeter, perhaps,.
for this long sleep of the spirit, and even
purer and fairer yet for a resurrection that
would veritably be as a new birth of soul and
intellect out of the blackness of the grave of
memory.

Falmouth, too, would possess for her scores
of points to touch her recollection with, and
vitalise it afresh. Especially did the thinker,
growing cheerier with his reflections, feel the
force of Stone's remark that the schooner
gave the girl no chance, if chance came not
to her in Fortescue himself, as he looked
along the decks of the gliding vessel and felt
the utter unfamiliarity of it all as presented
to her. Had the Golden Hope been an
Indiaman there might have been recognition

of her in Agatha, and the helpfulness of it ;
but what did he now see? A little craft, with
the moonlight empearling her canvas, the
rigging ruled in ebony lines upon those
delicately-tinted cloths, scarce less lovely with
their suggestions of dim, prismatic hues than
the fading lunar rainbow is; ivory decks, ex-
quisitely stained in deepest black by the outline of every object that threw a shadow; faint
silvery stars twinkling in the brasswork and
glass; a silent figure quietly moving here and
there in the shadows upon the forecastle; the
trucks soaring delicately and wanly on high
to the stars, under whose fiery hosts they
gently waved in unison with the breathing of
the ocean swell. It was a picture of repose,
of a heaven glorious with the lights of night;
and in the midst of it sailed the schooner, a
mere phantasm, floating forwards on wings
dim as mountain mist touched by starlight;
familiar to him, indeed now as familiar to
him as the fingers of his hand after all these
months ; for he had watched her often as he
had watched her now, in calm and in tempest, under the constellations which circled to
the north and to the south of the Equator;

and this watching of the schooner had raised in him an affection for the little vessel ; for she had borne them bravely, she had worked out his wonderful mission nobly, and he could not but feel a sailor's love for her, as though plank and beam, cordage and canvas and spar, were things of veins and pulses and heart, and could know human affection and respond to it.

Familiar to him as his fingers was the vessel, but not so to Agatha. There was no appeal to her in the Golden Hope, nor in the crew, nothing she could associate past fancies with. He felt that now that Stone had pointed it out to him, and the perception ran a thrill of hope through him, because it made him see that the girl's chances were yet to come.

It was half-past eleven ere he went below. He paused in the companion and said, "Good night, Mr. Stone."

"Good night, sir," answered the old fellow, touching his hat.

"Mr. Stone."

The seaman approached him.

"I've been turning over what you said.

Your words have given me a new heart. Strange that it should never have occurred to me to think of Miss Fox as capable of being influenced by associations apart from myself."

"'Tis the natural vanity we all has, sir," exclaimed Stone; "most of us is eat up by it. The finest natures has it. The sauce that is meant for relish very often spoils the meat it's put along with. 'Cause the lady don't recognise you, you've concluded that her memory's not to be got at. Now, you mark me, sir, and see if a little thing don't bring it back."

" Pray God your words may prove true," said Mr. Fortescue. "Good night, again, and thanks."

" Well, I've spoke out plain, and no mistake," said old Stone to himself as he walked over to the quarter, " but it's done him good, and so he ain't a-goin' to resent it. Preachin'! My precious eyes. Sure-ly a parson's calling must be a mighty easy 'un. Why, I could have given him a sarmon as long as the mainyard of a line-of-battle ship without drawin' a breath. Ay! and like the job, too.   Givin' advice makes a man feel important, and that's why, I suppose, we all finds it nicer to sarmonise than to be sarmonised." And so, talking to himself, the old fellow pulled a stick of tobacco from his pocket, out of which he bit a quid that effectually silenced his mutterings by obliging him to use his tongue to force it into his cheek.

CHAPTER IX

ALL night long the same quiet wind held. In the morning, with the rising of the sun, it freshened a trifle, and in the east the ocean was like molten silver with the trembling of the multitudinous surges which followed the schooner out of the south. It was like a promise of the trade-wind, this freshening of the draught, with its steady southern holding, as though it should veer eastward presently, and breeze up, strong and steady. Far off on the lee bow there was a glimpse to be had of a little barque bound northerly like the schooner, and resembling a fragment of crystal against the light blue sky of the horizon, otherwise the sea went bare to the sky, that was a brilliant dome overhead, full of fine weather.

After breakfast, the watch on deck turned

to their various duties. Stone strutted to and fro in the gangway, and the Golden Hope gathered a homeward-yearning look, from the smoke of her galley fire blowing over the bow, and from the distention of her canvas rounding forwards, and from the streaming of the little masthead vane, like a crimson flame against the blue, towards the north where the craft's home lay. The water slipped past prettily, and on Fortescue arriving from the cabin and asking the mate what the speed was, the log was hove, and the rate made five knots.

"It's her sharp lines with nothing to stop her in this smooth water, sir," said Stone. "Yet it's very delicate sailing to be sure; most choice. Them stunsails are doing the chief work; yet," said he, watching a bubble go by, "I never should have believed it to be five by merely looking."

"This will have been a long voyage," said the clergyman, with a half sigh, "by the time it is over. Few keep the sea for so many months as we have; but home will seem the sweeter and fairer for these weeks and weeks of dull salt water."

"Well, sir," responded Stone, "it'll no doubt seem an endless job to a gent like you who are not used to it ; but the woyage has answered our expectations, and if it had lasted six years instead of six months its tediousness should give us no call to grumble."

At this moment Agatha came on deck holding the baby. The cabin boy followed with a chair which Fortescue took and placed for her. She seated herself and he stood by her side.

In the searching morning light you would have noticed a marked expression, and yet a subtle one, too, in her face, to contrast with that air of new born beauty, like the second flowering of an exquisite plant, which she had stepped on board with from the island. There was a worn aspect that you found explained by the permanent wistfulness of her expression. Her white forehead showed signs of mental conflict. Without knowing the truth, you would have suspected, from the looks of her, that she was harassing her soul and dimming its divine light by religious dreads and doubts and worthless super-stitious conjectures. It was easy for For-

tescue to see how it was, though one thing
puzzled him greatly, too. Why, since Archer
had given her to know that she had a past
which was impenetrable to her, she should
not have fretted whilst on the island over
her incapacity to pierce the thing, as she
now grieved on board the schooner over
her helplessness? But then, had he not
told her what Archer never could have
hinted at? Had he not dwelt, again and
yet again, upon their betrothal, upon matters
which she would instinctively know to be
of priceless value to her, though they wore
no material shape, bore no material significance to her blinded light; forced her, by
his efforts to recall her memory, to dwell
upon what was hidden, as a mourner might
muse over something precious to the heart,
secreted by the ocean in a thousand fathoms
of dusky green obscurity? But for his passionate desire to flash the light of life into
her memory she might yet have retained
the sunny buoyancy and strange good spirits
and flushed improved beauty which had come
to her on the island. As he stood looking
at her, regret pierced his heart, for he had

grievously saddened without enlightening
her, and he feared in every drooping look,
in every broken sigh, in every feeble smile
fluttering quickly into fixity of sadness, the
approach of a form of inconsolable mania
which day and night he should know to be
owing to his own heedless eagerness that
her past should open to her.

She was warmly dressed, and she had
clothed the baby warmly, for the wind came
with a slight chill in it from the south, and
the sun was north of the Equator.

"It is wonderful," he said, kneeling in
front of the child to bring his face on a level,
and speaking with a perfect sweetness of
manner, and such a note of love that, observing there was no melting, no sparkling, no
glad nor gay response to it in the slow lifting
of her listless eye, you would have turned
away, touching your forehead, to another, as
an expression of your suspicion, "how you
have contrived to dress little Malcolm out of
the slender materials at your disposal. You
wield a magical needle, Agatha."

"It gives me occupation," she answered,
in a quiet voice, and as though she brought

her mind away from other thoughts with difficulty to attend to what he said. "Without my little boy this sailing, this constant sailing, would be very tiresome. I should pine for land—indeed, I do so greatly, but not as I should without my baby;" and she kissed him.

The little fellow began to talk to her in his way, raising his hands, and making to clutch at the sails as if he wanted them. She understood him, and answered, and presently quieted him by producing some trifle from her pocket.

"He is a beautiful boy," said Fortescue, who had been watching the little creature closely whilst he babbled to Agatha. "It is pretty sure to end in our having to adopt him, for there is nothing in the things found in the boat likely to yield a clue to his paternity, and he may go to his grave without ever knowing whose mother's son he is."

"I do not think I could part with him now, even to his mother, were she alive to claim him," said Agatha, putting her arm round the child and bringing him close to her with a quick impassioned clasp. "We have told

each other all our secrets. He knows my
heart—he knows my trouble."

Fortescue rose to his feet and said, "What
is *his* secret, Agatha?"

"Loneliness," she answered, looking down
at the boy.

"Ah! the same old fancy of yours, due to
the one haunting thought in you. But it is
not so, my darling. Consider, how can he be
lonely when he has your love, and how can
you be lonely when I am with you—I who
belong to the past which is yours, though for
a little while it is veiled—I who am visible
and real, though your mind's sight cannot
follow me beyond the moment of my coming
to you on the island. Oh, loved one! My
Agatha! Would to God that you could take
comfort! that I could give you comfort! that
you would think less, hope more, fear nothing,
believing me to be to you what I say I am,
trusting in me, therefore, and praying with me
for that light which in the Almighty's own
good time must dawn upon you."

The sinking eyelash, the sparkle behind it,
the sudden, quick rising and falling of her
bosom, warned him that he had said enough.

He went to the starboard bulwarks and stood, with his eyes fixed on the sea, thinking of her, asking himself whether it was possible that there was the power in the remembered sights and scenes, the familiar faces, the well-loved haunts of Wyloe, to touch her memory into life. If *not*, what would the end be? For if the faculty of recollection was veritably dead in her, killed by the miscreant that had been slain by Archer, could a new life, into whose composition there should enter the same elements that had been present in the past, be built upon that sandy plain of mind, under which lay crumbling the dead memorials of her existence as child, woman, and sweetheart?

But how could speculation avail him? He turned, bringing his eyes, dim with the thoughts that troubled and oppressed his heart, from the sea, but found that she had gone to the opposite rail, where she stood holding the infant, looking at the distant vessel. She had placed the child on the top of the bulwarks, holding him by the waist; and the clergyman's gaze lingered a moment or two, with love and sadness and

admiration mixed, upon the fair proportions
of his darling; for however hidden fretting
may have subdued the beauty in her face,
and sobered the dancing buoyancy of her
step, it had left unimpared the healthful and
free and graceful mien that to a large degree
—though a charming shape and lovely manner
were always hers—had been the gift of the
island, with its rosy sunlight glorifying the
warm blue serge that melted into silver about
her uncovered limbs, and its tropical climate
that had made the rags, in which her lover
had found her, clothing enough by day and
night, whilst fetterless as garments for her
beauty to ripen in ; her figure, grief had left
untouched, and he observed a gentle queenli-
ness of aspect in her at that moment, as she
stood holding the baby upon the rail, her
arms lifted, her hair looking like a soft glow
of light under the shadow of the hat she
wore, and the white of her throat and of her
arm, from the wrist to where the loose sleeve
exposed it below the elbow, giving back an
ivory dazzle of its own to the sunshine flowing down upon her, past the rounded cloths
of the mainsail.

He had glanced away again from her and
Stone, who was coming forward with a slow
step from the tiller, where he had been
addressing a few words to the helmsman,
when she uttered a scream that rang wild,
ear-piercing, with a note of inexpressible suffering in it, through the vessel, and swung
back from aloft in an echo that mingled at
the instant with the soft plash of a body
striking the water. In three bounds the
clergyman was at the girl's side, holding her
with a grip of steel, while she made frantic
efforts to climb over the bulwarks and plunge
into the sea. He had indeed saved her from
this act by scarcely more than the time it
takes for a man to fetch a breath. Her
shriek, that would have paralysed many, had
brought him to her side in the beat of a
heart, and he had her round the waist ere,
nimbly as she moved in her mad terror, she
had dragged herself half the height of the
bulwarks.

It had happened in a second, as all such
things do. The child, held erect upon the
rail, had suddenly made a plunge towards
some bubble or streak of sunlight upon the

passing water, and as the hold of the girl was slightly relaxed, with a mood of abstraction that had come upon her, the baby had freed himself from her clutch and sprang overboard.

"Hard down! Hard down!" roared Stone, pulling off his coat and flinging down his cap, and kicking off his boots with might and main as he bawled out the order; and the next thing Mr. Fortescue saw was the figure of the old fellow poised an instant upon the quarter, whilst he put his hands together like a man saying his prayers, to take the header. Splash! He vanished, and a whirl of bubbles came up where his heels had been. In a few seconds he re-appeared, blowing and fuming, with crimson countenance, his grey hair silvery upon the surface, striking out with grotesque and awkward gestures, but with steadiness and power, for the baby that lay face down, buoyed by its clothes.

Hiram came rushing on deck as though chased by fire. He had heard the shriek, and as he bounded through the companion he yelled out, "What is it? What is it?"

Fortescue, bringing the half-fainting girl away from the bulwarks, cried—

"The baby has fallen overboard, and Mr. Stone has jumped after him. They are just there!" and he pointed deliriously.

"Over with the boat, men!" cried Hiram, cooling quickly as his judgment and instincts as a seaman rose in him, toughening out his mind. "Out with that gangway, two of you! For God's sake, don't stand to cast them lashings adrift! Put your knives through 'em! Put your knives through 'em!"

The crew, at Agatha's shriek, had come together with a rush, bundling wildly out of the forecastle, those of them who were below, and gathering about the boat with amazing swiftness, they uprooted her, keel up as she lay in the bigger boat, ran her to the gangway, and in a trice had her overboard, launching her smack-fashion. Two men rolled into her, oars were flung to them and away they went to the speck, already a quarter-of-a-mile distant—so subtly swift was the schooner's sliding—that denoted old Stone nearing the baby, who lay motionless, always face downwards, now within a few strokes of his arm.

In a few minutes the two seamen, one of them standing up and rowing with his face forwards, were alongside; they dragged the old man in, streaming, and the little creature like a soaked rag lay motionless against his wet breast, as the boat danced back to the schooner. A half dozen hands received the child, and the mate followed. Agatha rushed forward.

"Give him to me," she cried in a voice raised almost to a scream. "My precious one! My little lamb!" And she pressed the dripping mite to her neck, leaning her chin upon its cheek and swaying to and fro with a motion of soothing that was full of anguish.

"Mr. Fortescue, quick, sir!" cried Stone, wringing the wet off his arms, "get the baby stripped and rolled in a blanket at once. No time must be lost. He's been floating on his face ever since he fell. Do ye know what to do to revive persons as seem drownded?" he said, speaking with vehement rapidity.

Fortescue helplessly shook his head.

"Then down with us, sir!" roared Stone,

and he made with rapid strides for the companion, whilst the clergyman, catching hold of Agatha, who seemed half stupified by the new fright that had come to her with the corpse-like stillness of the little body in her arms, hastened into the cabin after the old sailor.

Amongst them they rapidly unclothed the infant, and spread a blanket, and Stone, baring his arms and drying them, fell to turning the little thing about, working for artificial respiration, rubbing it and the like with evident knowledge of what was necessary, and using a hand that the bairn's mother would have kissed for the gentleness of its touch. It was a solemn sight, a most moving picture. Lifeless the baby lay, with ivory eyelids half raised, and glazing eyes looking, as it might seem, out of deepest sleep through the fringe of lashes. It was the creature's littleness that made its figure a sight to bring tears from a heart of stone. The bright hair was streaked and matted upon its head, but the lips wore yet their coral tint, and were parted, showing the few pearls; if aught of the duskiness of strangulation had entered the marble-like clearness of those baby features, the hue had passed away, and the face looked as it had ever seemed when the child slept sweetly, and the tranquil delight of pure slumber was in its expression. And then there was the broad, round-backed figure of old Stone, with eyes slowly moistening as the minutes passed and the child gave no sign ; there was this sturdy figure, with a pool of water at his feet, bending over the babe, his rugged features gathering an extraordinary accentuation of comely roughness from the refinement and beauty and delicacy of the tiny features he would often bend his mouth close to. There also was Mr. Fortescue, with a firm hold of Agatha's hand, standing erect with no other motion of his body than such as was communicated by the light swaying of the schooner, gazing with eyes full of earnest pity, in which the light of hope and the shadow of fear alternated, at the figure Stone was seeking to give life to ; and there was Agatha, tragical in her unconscious attitude of breathless eagerness and misery, suppressed but gnawing deep, the fingers of her free hand working convulsively, her breathing swift as a young child's, staring with startling intentness at the baby's face.

For a long while this went on, during which not a word was said ; then Stone, letting fall his hand, looked slowly round to Fortescue, manifestly afraid of Agatha's gaze, and exclaimed, in a voice but a little above a whisper, and with a long sigh breaking his sentence ; " I'm afraid, sir, the little un's drownded."

" Through me !" said Agatha, wresting her hand away from the clergyman's, and speaking in a tone that thrilled the hearts of both men. " It is God's will that I should remain alone. Oh! forgive me! Forgive me! My poor heart! My lost one ! My angel !" and as she said this she threw herself upon the little body, but with shining tearless eyes and after a wild wrestle for breath, fainted.

" It's as well it should happen so," said Hiram, who had come down softly and was looking on from the bottom of the steps, " 'tis but a swoon, Mr. Fortescue. Bill, I'll help to lay her down. You're all wet, mate, don't 'ee touch her. It's been a hard spin for you, but it was well done, ay, it was well done, matey. Oh! it's a cruel accident sartainly." And with every symptom of being deeply moved, Hiram helped Fortescue to lay the poor girl down upon a locker, and whilst the clergyman damped her cold forehead and loosened her collar, the skipper turned to the body of the little baby.

"Hiram!" said Stone, "afore I shift, let's put the poor little 'un away where she won't be able to see him, naked and miserable as he looks, when she comes to."

"Yes," said Fortescue, eagerly. "Clothe him as she would for the night, and place him in his crib and cover him up, Captain Weeks. It will seem more like his sleeping to her then, and the new shock that must come to her will be blunted a little."

Gently, and with a touching reverence of manner, Hiram raised the little body, and held it a minute, looking down into its face; then he shook his head, and as he did so a tear fell to the deck.

"To have saved ye for this, only!" he muttered, as he bore the dead infant into

Agatha's cabin. " Poor innocent ! It wasn't worth while ; it wasn't worth while !"

Between them they habited the tiny figure as the clergyman suggested, and placed it in its crib, laying it on its side so that the little face rested like an exquisite cameo upon the pillow. They drew the coverlet up to its neck, and softly pushing the crib to where the berth lay in the shadow, each man bent, one after the other, over the poor, nameless little corpse and kissed it, and then came out of the cabin on tip-toe.

CHAPTER X.

AN hour later Fortescue was sitting alone in the cabin, having left Agatha at her request. However affected he might have been by the sudden, violent death of the poor and nameless little creature that had come to them from out of the silence and mystery of the deep, his feelings now were with Agatha, whose grief was such that he could not think of it and be at the same time acutely sensible of the sudden extinction of the infant. Of course, he understood her sorrow.. It was not only that she accounted herself wholly responsible for the child's death by her heedless holding of it upon the rail —though that consideration alone might well make such a wound as would long keep conscience bleeding—the child had been her sole companion for weeks, her only occu-

pation, a light, even as of happiness, to
hinder the rapid rising and gathering of
gloomy sorrow begotten by realisation of
her mental blindness.

It must indeed be said that she had come
to love the boy as though he had been born
of her. The natural sweetness of her heart
would in any case have found in the innocence,
the youth, and the helplessness of the little
one, such an appeal to her affection as she
would have instantly answered. But her own
condition had put a deeper character than
mere womanly affectionate sympathy could,
into her feelings towards the child. How,
then, would this blow affect her? Mr. Fortescue thought, as he sat leaning his forehead
upon his hand, fresh from her presence. She
had looked at the little dead face with tearless eyes, when, having recovered from her
swoon, she was taken by the clergyman to
where the body lay; and whilst she remained
tearless, her lover viewed her furtively with
dismay, fearing the rigidity in her features,
and that pressure of her lips which held them
ashen. But before long she broke down,
wept piteously, kissed the lifeless bairn with a

kind of frenzy, violently upbraiding herself in broken sentences, and uttering a hundred moving things full of passion and misery.

He sought to comfort her, raising her hand to his mouth, smoothing her hair, filling up the pauses often rendered incoherent by failures of breath and long fits of sobbing, by endeavouring to make her understand that the child's death was an accident, and not owing to her; that bitter and hard to bear as the blow seemed, it was the act of God, to be resignedly borne; for who was to say, he urged, that the child's mother who had gone before, had not entreated for the soul of her child to be given her, and that the Creator, in mercy for the mourning spirit of the mother, and to spare the infant from that spiritual besoilment which must attend existence in the world and unfit it, perhaps, for Heaven, had hearkened to her prayer, and dispatched the messenger of death in the sacred name of divine compassion and in the not less sacred name of a mother's love?

Thus spoke the clergyman out of such metaphysical and yet material fancies as were sure to be inspired by his ardent and

imaginative faith.   But if she heard him
she did not seem to give much heed, till
at last when her sobs had calmed a little,
and there was a more tranquil expression
in her eyes, she asked him in a tremulous
whisper to leave her ; and he at once com-
plied.

Long before this, Stone had put on dry
clothes and returned on deck to his watch ;
but after Hiram had " made eight bells," the
old fellow came below, and finding Fortescue
alone, said, in a muffled voice and with a slow
look round, " How is she a-bearing of it, sir?"

" She remains quiet in her cabin," answered
Fortescue, " I do not care to intrude.   Let
me say now, as I should have said long ago,
Mr. Stone, how deeply your brave action,
in jumping overboard after the poor little
creature, has moved me."

The old sailor, giving a snuffle in his nose,
interrupted with a raised hand.

" Not a word on that subject, I beg of
you, sir.   Mr. Fortescue, I think ye are
wise in leaving her alone with the little 'un.
There's no tellin' what thoughts may visit
her.   I've been a-turning this lamentable

job over in my mind, and can't help fancy-
ing there may be a meaning wropped up
in it as'll come out plain to our sight by
waiting a bit. I dunno, I'm sure. There's
something so reemarkable in the whole of
this here woyage, that it looks to me as if
nothen could happen but that it is meant
to sinnify more than 'ud appear in it on
any other occasion. Why should that there
little baby be drownded, Mr. Fortescue?
What hurt had he done? I tell ye what,
sir, if we're to judge of things only as we
sees them, in their literal shapes, without
viewing of them as seeds out of which
there's a-going to be a growth by-and-bye,
why, then, the sooner we tarns to and con-
siders that it's the devil as made this here
universe and has got hold of the tiller and
is a-governin' of us, the better. That's Bill
Stones's notion, and I ain't ashamed to say
it to a clergyman."

But Mr. Fortescue was in no humour to
reason. Probably he might have agreed with
the sailor. Whilst they conversed, his ear
was bent towards the door of Agatha's berth,
and his glance often wandered that way. To

him, as to old Stone, the notion had come that
the girl's watching and mourning by the side
of the little corpse might lead to thoughts, to
impulses, to emotions which should be as
memory's dawn to her—turning her blackened
mind, though but with a little movement only,
towards the light which yet, through the
mental inclination, should cast the paleness
of a sunrise not far off upon an atmosphere
that was now an impenetrable obscurity.

"As you said yesterday," exclaimed Fortescue, thinking aloud, "a little thing may
do it."

"Ay, sir, a little thing ; and perhaps the
very last the most h'energetic fancy would
be likely to imagine. Will ye keep the
body long, sir ?"

"I must be advised by you and Captain
Weeks. What is the usual course, Mr.
Stone ?"

"Why, as there ain't a shadow of a doubt
that the poor fellow is dead, there's no cause
to keep him an hour longer than ye choose.
It's a job which ye can't get too soon done
with ; besides, sailors have a superstition agin
sailing with corpses. They like to feel they're

overboard — even a poor little baby's like this."

"It might shock Miss Fox," said the clergyman, "if the funeral were hasty. Would the crew object to our waiting till the morning?"

"Why, no, of course they wouldn't. I shouldn't have thought myself of naming an earlier time. To-morrow, at six bells, sir. That'll be eleven o'clock in the forenoon watch, if Captain Weeks is agreeable. He must be buried as a sailor, sir," said the old man, with a mist coming over his eyes, though he looked at the clergyman steadfastly. "There ain't a question in my mind of his having been a sailor's son, and his last toss must be conducted on that idea. I've got the afternoon below, and I'll make him a proper little hammock, with clews to hold a sinker, sir," said the old fellow, sniffing as he spoke, "and when stitched up, Mr. Fortescue, and lying on a plank, with the ensign over him, he'll look as his own father could have wished to see him at such a time. It'll be my job, only I wish ye'd manage to draw Miss Fox out of the berth whilst I takes the little chap's measure, for the hammock musn't be too small, and it won't look ship-shape if it's too large."

At this point Hiram came below. Stone repeated to him the suggestions he had made to Mr. Fortescue, and, the skipper consenting, the matter was settled.

All the afternoon, in the cabin, with a pair of spectacles on, a sailmaker's palm in his hand, and a gleaming needle between his fingers, old Stone sate bending over pieces of sail-cloth, which he was stitching into a hammock for the baby to be buried in. There was little need for him to take the trouble he did. A plain piece of canvas would have sufficed; but it was not only that the old man had come to love the little boy, he believed him to be a sailor's son, and with the proud sympathy that all genuine Jacks have with their calling and those who form it, he was determined that the sea shroud in which the little one was to go to his ocean grave should be such as the most critical mariners would declare fit and becoming. When he had done he called to Mr. Fortescue, who brought Agatha from her berth, telling her what Stone wanted to do there.   It was late in the afternoon ; the girl had exhausted her tears, and she came out quietly with the clergyman, and went on deck with him.   Stone entered the berth and did his work there, but it was a task that came very near to breaking him down more than once.   Often during the long years he had spent at sea, he had lent a hand to stitch up in canvas the remains of shipmates ; but then they had always been men — rough, sturdy fellows in life ; and though the disease they had died of might have wasted them, yet he could recollect them starting as active, hearty sailors, who had lived, and who, if death had come to them prematurely, were still not so young as to make the visit seem cruel for its earliness.   But when he raised the tiny form and laid it in the little hammock, the soft-hearted old fellow could have wept like a woman.   The half-opened eyes seemed to follow him as though they thanked him for his tenderness, and for his brave plunge overboard in the morning.   He kissed the cold forehead, passed his fingers through the yellow hair, and with an involuntary look up to God as if the hiding of the body in the hammock was like the act of giving it to Heaven, he fell to stitching the canvas along, and soon the little form lay encased, ready for the morning.

When this was completed, the old man stepped on deck and motioning so as to bring Mr. Fortescue near to Hiram, he said that the body was stitched up in the hammock, "and I think now," added he, "for the sake of the lady it had better be taken forward and covered over with a tarpaulin."

"Yes," said Fortescue, "I should not like it to be all night in the same berth with Miss Fox."

"No hurt can come to it," said Hiram, "in this quiet weather, with a tarpaulin over it. As ye say, Bill, it's best taken forward."

Stone went to the flag locker, a box in which a little show of bunting was kept, and taking out the small ensign, stepped below with it, and reverently wrapping the hammock up in the colour, he brought his burthen on deck, holding it in his arms as if it were a sleeping infant he was hushing to

his heart. When Agatha saw him emerge
from the companion-way, and observed what
he held, she started violently and half rose
from her chair; but Fortescue grasped her
hand and stood in front of her, whereupon
she fell back, hiding her eyes, but she did
not speak. Stone was bareheaded, and
Hiram as he passed pulled off his cap, as
did Archer, who was at the tiller. Forward,
the men went on with their various jobs,
glancing at what lay in Stone's arms, and
then addressing themselves afresh to what
they were about; those who had tobacco in
their mouths chewed perhaps with increased
energy, and in all of them you saw a soberness of expression entering their faces, like a
deeper dye in the mahogany of their cheeks.
Placing the body upon the deck, Stone drew
over it a tarpaulin, which he secured at the
corners, and there, ready for the morning,
lay all that was mortal of the little waif
whom the old seaman had declared to be a
sailor's son, but whose paternity was now to
be a mystery that should outlast the world,
and be without determination till He who
loved little children and called them unto

him, and who had declared that of such as
this innocent boy was the Kingdom of
Heaven, should come to judge the living and
the dead.

These, at least, were Mr. Fortescue's
thoughts as he watched Stone. He sought
to soothe Agatha, but she did not seem
able to listen to him. If ever she spoke
it was only to mutter in broken speech that
she was answerable for the child's death,
and that that thought would make her loneliness more than she could bear. After a
while she said that the sunshine pained
her eyes, and asked Fortescue if she might
go to her cabin, speaking as though she
had no will of her own, and with a note
of grief in her voice that harshened its
sweetness, and with a manner that almost
neutralised the particular loveliness of bearing which had marked the timidity she was
wont to address him with, after she had
got to learn, as though by rote, what he had
told her about their being betrothed, and
how they were to be married when they
reached England.

The evening came along with the same

quiet wind that had been blowing all day whispering through it, with purple splendours swiftly fading in the west, and the stars eastward flashing quickly into their places, for there was but a narrow interval of twilight, and in those latitudes the night will be striding across the deep when the waters facing the direction whence she rises still wear the hectic of the vanished luminary. The crew gathered about the forecastle and talked in low voices. The little creature that in life had been a toy for the men to look at with amused and sympathetic faces was now a mighty power to subdue them; wizard-like, filling the air with the shadow of death, so that the mysterious influence coming from it touched and gloomed in all that the sailor's eyes rested upon, putting a deeper darkness upon the ocean, a pallider light upon the bosom of the sails sleeping to the sighing of the wind, a meaning, not at any other time to be caught, into the soft sobbing of the water, broken by the stem into lines in which the reflection of each star broadened as it rode over the long ripple.

Fortescue paced the quarter-deck, too much

absorbed in thought for conversation with Hiram, whose watch it was, and who talked in a low voice with Duck, who was at the tiller. Stone came up to smoke. He took a few turns in the gangway, then stepped forward to see that all was right with the tarpaulin, and observing the men grouped forward of the forerigging, talking, he joined them. As beforesaid, there was not the discipline of a ship aboard the little schooner. Hiram and Stone were no better than others of the crew, though of course they were obeyed and were men whom the sailors had signed articles to sail under as captain and mate ; yet, they had been careful to keep at their end of the craft during the voyage, and the mate joining the seamen now was felt as a sort of condescension and kindness on his part, and when he stepped amongst them there was silence, meant as a sign of respect.

" It is a sad business, the little 'uns death," said he, putting his back against the rail, and folding his arms, and casting his gaze aloft while he sucked at his pipe.

" There will be no more stopping," exclaimed Goldsmith, emptying his pipe by striking it on the palm of his hand so as to make no noise, "as a chap comes forward after his trick to tickle of him under the chin and make him smile. It'll be something to miss. He had a way of hoisting up whatever he might be a-playing with to show it ye, that made a man feel like as if he'd been saying of a prayer, ay, and feeling of it too. What's there to snigger at in that, I should like to know, cook?"

"There's no sniggering in me," answered the cook. "It's Johnny snuffling."

This was accepted as the fact, because Johnny did not deny the charge. The men's faces glimmered very feebly to the starlight, and it was impossible to note expressions.

"When a little chap like that there dies," said the cook, "what becomes of him?"

"Tarn to and read the Bible and find out," answered Stone, gruffly, but in a low voice. "There's no call of being afraid of over-h'educating yourself in that direction, Micky."

"Well, I don't know," exclaimed Breeches. "I was acquainted with a man as owned to belonging to a religious party what call themselves the Select."

"The Elect ye mean, perhaps," said Archer.

"Well, the H'elect then. This chap said he knew where he was a-goin' to. He was called, and was bound to be a h'angel. There was nothen as could stop him. The Lord had got hold of his helm, and he was holding a course for Heaven true as a hair. That was the result of spiritoal over-h'education, boys. He kept all on readin' and readin' about souls and how they're saved and the like, till he drifted into a regular ocean of ideas, with such a sea running that his ballast shifted, and there he was with a strong list, everything wrong, rudder gone, compass overboard, everything adrift, and him all the while cock-sure and not doubtin' that if he could only see under his shoulder-blades he'd find the wings a-sprouting."

"I agrees with William," remarked Kitt, meaning by William, Breeches. "There," said he, pointing with a shadowy arm in the direction of the tarpaulin, "lies one as never thought, yet as compared with *his*

chances, I should like to know what 'ud
be those of the larnedest man as ever
studied hisself into becoming boss of all
the parsons, Bishop o' Canterbury, or whatever the name is?"

" Well, 'tain't a subject for argufication,"
said Stone.   " 'Arry, slacken that wang a
trifle.   Where are we going to pick up the
trade-wind, I wonder?"

" This drownin' job isn't going to do
the lady much good, I doubt," exclaimed
Breeches.   " She's an astonishin' mystery
to me, Mr. Stone.   It's onderstood her
mem'ry's gone; which bein' so, how is it
everything isn't strange to her? How can
she tell where her hair is, what to do with
her boots, how to use a knife, how to reck'lect
the names of things she asks for, like water,
or bread, or tea?   Why, she dressed the little
'un from head to foot; how could she ha'
done it without mem'ry?"

" You must always consider, Bill," said the
cook, speaking in a tone manifestly depreca-
tory of any observation he might challenge
from Stone, " that this lady may not have
been cast in the exact resemblance of other

folks. A party as is never more rational than when she ain't got her intellects, which are usually reckoned to be sealed up when people are asleep," he added, referring to her sleep-walking, "may set ye a-wondering, but she'll defy ye to explain her."

"Look here, Micky," said Stone, "when ye've had enough of cookin', mate, you tarn to an' become a nat'ral ph'losopher. A man as can 'splain a thing by showin' it ain't 'splainable's goin' to save money for his old age, an' as ph'losphy's your *forty* don't ye keep your prospects a-waitin'. The fact is, Bill," said he, addressing Breeches, "the more ye think of what's called the human mind the less ye can make of it; consequently I'm for taking all wonderful things as happens as they come, just as ye look at them there stars; satisfied to notice that they're bright without troubling to consider how it is that if they're made of earth like this here globe they sparkles like polished silver. There's no use in dropping a lead overboard and keeping all on paying out line when ye know there is no soundings to be got. Here and there life shoals and ye get bottom;

but it's mostly so deep that I tell ye the
furdest of them stars up there ain't furder
off than the ocean-bed of existence is from
the reach of our knowledge. Respecting
Miss Agatha Fox," he continued, speaking
with the complacency he must inevitably
feel from the flattering silence that attended
his speech, "it's like this to my notion;
and I'll explain my idea in what they calls
a h'allegory. Ye can't understand how it
is she's got a recollection of things she asks
for, like when she calls for bread, or a knife,
or a fork, or hunts about for cotton to thread
her needle with. Well, this is my view.
Take a man with one blind eye, t'other eye
being all right; and now imagine that this
here man isn't able to turn his head on the
side his blind eye is. Well, now it stands to
reason that if his werry oldest friend was to
sheer alongside of this blind eye the man
wouldn't know him, for the simple reason that
he couldn't see him. All on the blind side
'ud be darkness. On t'other side he could
see what was happening, and owing to the
wision being of such a nature that if a man
stares straight ahead he'll see more things

than he looks at, by side objects coming into
the range of his sight, he might be able to
perceive with the good eye just a little of
what 'ud come into the circle of the blind eye
if it could see. That's a h'allegory answering
to Miss Fox's case. One side of her brain's
in darkness. It's like a blind eye turned on
whatever comes before it. T'other side's all
right, and's got the power of taking in a little
of what 'ud fall into the spear of the dark
side, if that dark side was alive and sensible.
Small things, like needles, and corfee and the
like, are within that spear, and the right side
of her onderstanding catches hold of 'em; but
big affairs, which needs her full brain to see,
are invisible to her. So there ye have it
'splained in a h'allegory, Bill; but I don't
mean to say it ain't puzzling, all the same."

Breeches grunted as though satisfied, but
some hoarse whispered comments were uttered
by the others, which must have plunged all
hands into a long discussion, had Stone been
impolitic enough to overhear them. Soon
again, however, the subtle, subduing influence created by the little silent body under
the tarpaulin was felt by the men. Their

thoughts went to the infant, and they spoke
of him ; then Martin Goldsmith remembered
a creepy and chilly story of an apprentice
who had been an orphan, and was put to
sea by an uncle whom he had talked of as
a harsh and cruel man. This lad died
through a fall from the masthead. They
laid him out, and that same night an able
seaman named Moses Bogles, going aft to
take the wheel and passing by where the
body lay, saw the apparition of a female
with her fingers locked upon her forehead,
leaning over the body and suggesting by
her attitude that she had discovered who
the boy had been, and was in wild anguish.
" Bogles was so frightened," said Goldsmith,
" that he ran back again into the fo'ksle, and
woke up all hands, who came on deck to see
the apparition, but the figure had disappeared.
Yet there was not the least doubt that
Bogles had spoken the truth, for his
sincerity was shown by the effect the
sight produced upon his mind. He had
been a drunken, swearing fellow before, but
from that night he read the Bible regularly
and became a pious man." Anson, the cook,

had also his little yarn to deliver; Archer likewise told of a ghost, and old Breeches, never to be beaten when it came to spinning twisters, narrated in a gruff but tremulous voice how his mother had been visited in the dead of night by an elder brother of his, who came to the street door when the snow was a foot thick, with nothing on but a pair of drill trousers. "There was a moon," said Bill, "and she saw his face plain, but as she'd only received a letter a fortnight afore—he was in the Royal navy, was Joseph — saying that the frigate had reached Kingston, Jamaica, and was like to be kept on that there station for some months, she was so confounded, not more by his turning up in that rig than by his turning up at all, that she tumbled down in a fit, the noise of which, alarming a lodger that had a wooden leg, who slep' in the back parlour, he shipped his leg and came out, and seeing nothen but mother a-laying in a swound upon the mat, he shuts the street door and carries her on to a sofa, where, after a bit, she rewived. Well, what happened?" said old Breeches turning his face, dim in the starlight, round upon the men, the glistening of whose eyes was the only discernible point in their dusky countenances. "Some time after, she got a letter from the Admiralty, stating that her son Joseph had been drownded by falling overboard at night in Kingston harbour, and it tarned out that at the very time he was under water the knock came at the door, and mother see him a-standing in the snow."

But it was hard upon eight bells; Stone had finished his pipe, and drawing himself up with a look round at the sea, he said, "Well, we live in a fantastic world, but there's no use a-growling;" and with that he walked quietly aft, pausing a moment when abreast of the tarpaulin and looking at it, and then moving on afresh with a sigh. The men after talking a little broke up. The first watch had begun; half the crew went below, the others, who had to keep the deck, hung together, walking in twos and twos, one pair in the gangway, another in the forecastle. The shadow of death was on the little ship, and where the tarpaulin was the darkness hung deep, and as often as the spot was passed the footfall was softened, the low voice sunk lower yet into a whisper. It would be mere imagination, of course ; yet the whole thing appeared as though accentuated by the night ; by the steady, solemn burning of the stars ; by the delicate swell that underran the schooner with a melancholy respiration ; by the parting waters stealing along in sounds of weeping ; by the spectral wings of canvas slowly fanning the darkness under the glittering heights ; by the light moaning noises breaking out from God knows what part of the interior of the gliding fabric.

Even to thee, oh, tiny fragment of human clay, there had come the marvellous gift of death ; the power of subduing to the complexion of its inspirations whatever the eye could behold, whatever the ear could hear.

.   .   .   .

The wind shifted in the night. It blew, but without much weight, from the north, and the sun rose upon the Golden Hope close-hauled, leaning slightly, three points off her course. Fortescue, who, in accordance with his regular custom, had turned the key in Agatha's door overnight—with greater solicitude on the occasion than he had before felt, for he greatly feared the perturbing influence of the sorrowful events of the day upon her mind and the domination of sorrow not less active in sleep than in waking — Mr. Fortescue, on quitting his own berth, lightly unlocked her door, and after listening intently for some moments, knocked. She answered by opening the door. She was fully dressed, but had not yet bound her hair up; it was like a sun-touched fountain raining down her back and over her shoulders, wondrously plentiful and most daintily rich and radiant; her beauty, pale and hard with melancholy—with such melancholy as would possess a mind that was without memory, without a remembered past and the solace retrospection yields—met the vision of the lover with the novelty he would have found in a marble image of his darling. There was a darkness under the ever gentle eyes, a languor in the droop of the lids which told of a troubled night. He held her hand as he asked her how she had slept.

" Not well," she answered ; " I missed my little companion "—her lip quivered.

" Why, that was to be expected, Agatha," he said, calling her by her name, for there was something in the stoniness grief had put into her face, that to his sensitiveness repelled the more endearing terms he was used to employ ; " but time, that heals all, will soon accustom you to the poor babe's absence."

She looked down as though she disdained such an assurance as that, and said with scarcely moving lips, like one thinking aloud, " I caused his death. It was intended it should be so. Why was memory taken from me if it was not meant I should be alone— alone !" She raised her hand as though to press her forehead, but touching her hair she seemed startled to find it hanging wild about her, and with a faint blush of confusion she made as though to close the door upon the clergyman.

"Will you come to the table to breakfast, Agatha, or shall I bring a tray here to you ?"

" I will come to the table," she answered.

He said softly, " The little one will be

buried at eleven.   Is it your wish to be present?"

"Yes," she responded, with an unusual quickness, turning towards him. "Certainly, I wish to be present."

Her manner checked him, otherwise he might have asked her to consider whether she would have the heart to witness the slipping of the little hammock off its plank, and to bear the gaze of the men, all of whom would be assembled. She came to the breakfast-table when the meal was ready, but only responded very faintly and briefly to Hiram's respectful salute.   Seeing it was not her humour to speak, Weeks fell silent himself, and breakfast was got through with scarce more than a half-dozen of words between the skipper and Mr. Fortescue.   Her manner was a blow to Weeks, who had been rehearsing many observations of a consolatory character.   The truth is, he considered that William Stone had enjoyed too large a share of the privilege of advising the clergyman, and sermonising both him and Miss Fox as occasion required.   He felt that his own parts in this respect would remain unimagined

if he did not brush up the mind God had
given him, and deliver the opinions which
formed in him during his watch on deck, or
his waking moments below. However, there
was no help for it. The inexpressible something in Agatha's face and bearing that had
silenced even in Fortescue the impassioned
loving names he had hitherto called her by,
was acutely felt by Weeks also, as he sat
working away at a plate of rashers of bacon,
with a hasty ogle of her from time to time out
of the corner of one protruding eye.

When breakfast was over she rose quietly,
passing near the clergyman to say, "Will you
let me know when I am to come on deck for
the funeral?"

"Certainly," he answered.

Thereupon she went straight to her berth.
Hiram standing erect on his compass-like
legs, looked intently at Fortescue, as though
debating whether he should speak; but it was
impossible for him to keep his tongue still.
He said, in a harsh, saw-like whisper:—

"Never could have believed, sir, she had
so taken to that there child. Had she been
its own mother, the drowning of it couldn't

have caused her more grief. Pity it happened
all this way down here. It wouldn't so much
matter if this sorrow had fallen upon her when
we was even within a week's sail of England,
for then there'd be all the interests of the
shore close at hand to smother down her
lamentations a bit and, may be, as Bill
Stone thinks, to give her back her memory;
in which case the joy she'd find in recollecting of 'ee and beholding once again all them
old satisfactions which she can't now perceive, would make this melancholy little job
seem small enough, though such is the
natural gentleness of her heart that I don't
mean to suppose she wouldn't always find
it affecting."

Fortescue had too sweet a nature ever to
show impatience at the good intentions of
others, no matter how distressing might be
the form they took ; but Agatha had inspired
him with thoughts infinitely too deep for
utterance to such a man as Weeks, and with
fancies and fears which made him recoil from
the mere idea of talking about her. Weeks'
ambition to shine as a philosopher and a
moralist must therefore be baulked again.

The clergyman, with a bit of commonplace on his lips which, strive his utmost, he could not force into a smile, went to his berth, and Hiram, passing the back of his hand with a long sweep over his mouth, and with a slightly crestfallen look, fitted a moleskin cap to his head and climbed on deck to relieve old Stone.

The morning passed quickly. It was now a quarter to eleven. The men were below in the forecastle, cleaning themselves for the ceremony; the young seaman, Joe Hall, was at the tiller, and Stone, in his Sunday clothes, paced the deck with a sober, pious look upon his face. The schooner, heeled to the extent of a strake by the breeze, was sailing quickly but without noise, for the sea was smooth, and what small billows the wind set running were but little more than large ripples, with curls of foam flashing out of their heads, here and there, too light to break with sound against the weather bow.

There was no bell to strike, but at eleven o'clock the word went along, and the crew lay aft, collecting at the gangway, whither one of them came—no other than William

Breeches—bearing under his arm a plank
with the little body upon it, over which was
spread the English ensign. One end of this
plank he rested on the rail, the other he held.
He was bareheaded and kept his rugged,
weather-seamed face bowed. They had, these
plain merchant-sailors, but little choice of
clothes among them ; their mourning must
be gotten out of polished faces and hair
combed smooth, and clean shirts washed in
salt water, and, some of them, canvas trousers
whose tarry stains defied the scrubbing-brush
and the lee scuppers. They were promptly
joined by Hiram and Stone, the former, like
his mate, clad in his best suit. Upon the
skipper's long, gaunt, yellow face, grief, of a
mute-like type, was nicely calculated to sit
becomingly ; but had he been acting sorrow
all his life, no expression of it he could have
assumed could come near to a likeness of the
manly, pathetic honesty of feeling you saw in
his eyes, when after letting them rest for a
few moments on the little burden, he turned
them upon the deck at his feet, gazing so till
he had tautened his wide mouth out of the
twitchings in the extremities of it.

In a few moments Fortescue came out of
the companion with Agatha.   The clergyman
took his place close to the body.   The men
backed away a little to make room, particularly leaving a space for Agatha, facing the
gangway.   Her face was painfully white ;
the most ignorant glance would have traced
the marks of the grief the loss of the child
had impressed upon her.   The hollows in
her eyes were noticeable for the darkness in
them, and for the aspect of illness they gave
to her.   It was difficult to look at her and
not observe the fading that had happened in
twenty-four hours, without guessing that there
had been an artificiality in her island bloom,
in that warm, flushed, tropic glow of beauty
which had amazed Fortescue to see in her and
which had lingered scarce unimpaired, down to
the last week or two, when it began to dim,
to her secret fretting.   She fixed her eyes
on the ensign that covered the plank, and
seemed utterly insensible to all things but the
fancies that came to her from the outline
defined by the thin bunting.   The sailors
looked at her slightly ; their respect was too
strong to suffer their glance to approach a

stare, and then again it was a moment to subdue them and to sharpen their natural regret at the loss of the little one whom they had watched, talked to and learned to love, into briny pity and a rough sort of grief. Still, they could not help peeping at her, for she stood near; her colourlessness and fixed gaze, her still, wrapt posture, invited their regard. It is true that Archer had cleared their minds of the superstition she had excited in them, but the memory of the fancies they had had about her recurred. This was the girl, some of them thought in their own rude tongue, who had been beheld by that clergyman yonder, when at a distance of thousands of miles from her, kneeling upon the shore of the island, then rising and appealing to him to come to her; from whom sickness had fallen as a garment, after memory had been shocked out of her by brutality; whose past had blackened upon her mind and was as dead to her as the infant upon the plank there, though in sleeping she could recollect, and standing under the starlight at the rail of the schooner look across the rounded sea to England from the Indian Ocean, and talk with her lover as

if he were there instead of being at her side,
and appeal to him as if there was no sanity
for her but in slumber, though when she
opened her eyes in waking she turned them
like a blind woman upon him!

The schooner swayed gently; at every
man's foot his shadow swung, and in the
pause that fell, whilst Fortescue opened his
book ere raising it to read, you would have
heard nothing but the innumerable whisper-
ings of the water, delicately seething and
softly sliding past, as though there were
spirits over the side answering in faint notes
the muffled questionings of the winds, that
hummed like the buzzing of flies heard afar
amid the complicated cordage, and past the
bolt ropes of the steady cloths.

Mr. Fortescue began to read. It was a
familiar office to him, and his voice was low,
steady and sad, but sweet with cultivated
utterance. The moment he commenced,
Breeches quietly pulled the ensign off the
little hammock, ready for the final launch,
since he could not imagine when the word
would be given, having but the very
slenderest acquaintance with the burial ser-

vice, and therefore seeing "everything clear,"
as a true sailor should, under all circumstances.   It was noticed that a shudder
wrenched Agatha from head to foot, that her
fingers closed into the palms as if the nails
would cut the flesh there, and that she let a
breath fly from her in a passionate sigh, that
was like a faint cry to those who stood
nearest, when the hammock was exposed ;
otherwise she held herself steady with her
eyes rooted upon the little body.

But it was indeed a sight to melt any
heart.   Never had the blue of heaven
looked down upon a tinier hammock.   In
its littleness mainly lay the appeal that
stirred the men when the old seaman laid
bare the minute ocean-shroud.   Old Stone's
eyes were wet, Hiram folded his arms
tightly across his breast and hung his head,
and Archer, after a short look at the baby
outline, turned his head aside with his hand
over his face.

Mr. Fortescue continued reading slowly,
with a thrill running through his voice for
a moment as he lifted his eyes from the
book and directed them at the plank, but

old Stone was observed to suddenly squeeze a knuckle into his eyes and regard Agatha askant, but with a steadfast watchfulness of gaze that must have made you see his mind was wholly off the funeral, and that he was thinking of nothing but what he looked at.

A change had come over her, too. She had broken away from her intent stare at the baby, and was now gazing at Mr. Fortescue, with a singular expression slowly entering her face and stirring in every twitch and line of it, and gradually dilating her eyes and lifting her brows like a slow poison of madness working in her brain. No one appeared to notice this but Stone.

Mr. Fortescue read: "*We therefore commit his body to the deep to be turned into corruption.*"

He paused, with a glance at Breeches, which the old man instantly understood. With a quick movement he raised the end of the plank, and the tiny white hammock flashed from the rail like a bird of snowy plumage taking flight. Hall, at the tiller, instinctively turned his head to look over the quarter, but the passing water, sobbing along the bends, had caught the bubble and swept it into the sunshine in the wake, and in a breath it was gone, symbolising the vanishment of the little one in a manner fit truly to deepen the hope expressed in the words, *"looking for the resurrection of the body (when the sea shall give up her dead), and the life of the world to come, through our Lord Jesus Christ."*

The clergyman was proceeding, solemnity gathering in his rich voice now that the plank had been tilted, and the feeling was that the nameless little stranger that had come to them for their love and ministration was at last truly at peace, and in the bosom of Him who had called him, when, on a sudden, Stone cried out, " Mr. Fortescue, look at Miss Fox, sir !"

She was standing as though transfixed, with an expression on her of wildest astonishment, that of its own emotional force had given a colour to her face and brought the blood to her cheeks. Her eyes were opened to their fullest extent. It was as if a spirit moved before her—something that had at

first filled her with an amazement like horror,
though the terror was passing, and the lustre
of delight was dimly sifting through the
astonished, half incredulous, half terrified
stare that she had fixed upon her lover. She
tottered once or twice as if she would fall.
She sought to speak, but her lips turned
white with the effort, and her throat crimsoned
as with strangulation ; but ere Mr. Fortescue
could spring towards her, she had uttered his
name. " Malcolm !" at first in a choking cry,
but then, " Malcolm ! Malcolm ! Malcolm !"
thrice, in shrieks ; and with a leap she was
upon his breast, her hands locked round his
neck, her head upon his bosom.

"Agatha," he cried, "you know me at last !
Your memory has returned to you ! Beloved
one ! Call me again by name !"

Her clasp relaxed. She fainted.

" 'Tis the baby's doing," said Stone, aloud,
looking round; "she loved him, and he repays
her by giving her her memory back. It came
with the launching of the hammock. I
watched it working in her. Great God !
how beautiful it is to think of a woman's
happiness returning to her as a gift of love

from the little 'un she'd been as a mother to!" And with working lips and eyes again brimming over, the old man stepped to the rail, and looked along the glittering furrow of the schooner towards the spot where the body of the little one had vanished.

CHAPTER XI

THE NEW DAWN.

IT was the girl's second swoon in twenty-four hours, but this time there was a death-liness in it that grew terrifying. The ashen pallor was of the grave, and through the parted lids the white of the eyes showed like that of a corpse. For a moment or two Fortescue alone knew she had fainted, then Hiram, seeing what had happened, sprang to help him, and between them they bore her below.

The momentary transport of joy in the curate turned to terror as he leaned over her, loosening her dress whilst Hiram hurried for water and other restoratives. She was pulseless. Her bosom lay motionless as a piece of sculpture. He drew forth with trembling hand a little looking-glass which he held to her lips, but it remained un-tarnished. It was as sure as that the child

was dead, as that the schooner was upon the
sea, as that the heavens looked down upon
all, that she had recognised him, and that
her memory had therefore returned. Was it
possible that the mad leap of the revitalised
faculty from the tomb in her brain in which
it had been lying dead had broken her heart?
Sudden joys, sudden griefs have been known
to kill, but think of the power, the force of
the emotions which must have swept into her
with lightning swiftness, when the curtain
was dropped from her mind and her lover
stood before her!

Minute after minute went by. Ceaselessly
the curate moistened her brow, chafed her
hand, did what he knew, with a prayer to
God going up in every breath that left him;
whilst Hiram, grasping a stancheon, stood
erect, mute and waiting. A whole half-
hour passed, as full, to the clergyman, of
misery as a lifetime of suffering could have
contained, and to the seaman steadfastly and
silently watching, of deeper anxiety than he
had ever felt in the wildest weather at sea.
Then on a sudden they heard a faint sigh,
her fingers twitched, something of living

colour entered palely into her white lips. A sigh again broke from her, this time like the respiration of one dreaming sorrowfully in sleep.   She opened her eyes, looked strangely about her as though her rest had been induced by a powerful narcotic, until her sight coming to Mr. Fortescue, an expression of wonder, delight, amazement, brightened in them, and she suddenly sat erect, crying yet again with hands extended to him, "Malcolm! Malcolm! My Malcolm!"

He took her in his arms; he could not speak; his full heart gave way and he wept with his face against her cheek as he held her to him.   Captain Weeks walked to the companion and stood mid-way on the steps with his head outside the hatch, where he was within call, though he could not hear their conversation, and where he could act as sentinel.   Fortescue mastered his deep agitation after a little, but until he did so she did not move.   She felt his need of concealing his face whilst he strove with his tears, and even in that marvellous moment of the return of memory, and whilst still fresh and confused from her swoon, she soothed him

with her cheek to his, and left the sweet
pillow of her shoulder motionless for his comfort. But the instant he stirred, as if to lift
his head, she started from his embrace, and,
seizing his hands, fell back to the length of
her arms with a long, yearning, searching look
at his face—a wondrous stare for eyes so soft
and gentle as hers to fix, so full was it of
astonishment, inquiry, passionate delight,
conflicting with incredulity and breathless
amazement.

"Malcolm!" she said, in a low voice that
thrilled with the feelings which her eyes
looked ; "Malcolm!" she repeated, in a
tone that deepened as it sank towards a
whisper, "is it you, dearest one, is it *you*,
my own, from Wyloe? Where am I?
This is a ship ; it is not the island." She
looked slowly around, labouring to master
the meaning of what she saw, till she brought
her eyes to rest again upon her lover. "Malcolm," she continued, letting fall his hand to
press her forehead with a gesture she had
often used since she had been on board
the schooner, "have I been sleeping? Do
I still sleep, and dream?" An expression of

terror now swept across her face, obliterating its bright expression of intelligence, and she rolled her eyes hysterically.

Fortescue saw the task before him.   He had a will that had served him well on more than one occasion.   He exerted it to thrust down out of sight the emotions which had overwhelmed him, and his fine intellect went swiftly to work to consider how he should act, how he should deal with the delicate, bewildering, dangerous problem that Agatha's condition of mind submitted.   The *whole* truth might craze her ;   he must speak with the utmost caution, for the present at least, since it was possible that the faculty of memory might prove weak and treacherous after its long stupor ; and it was certain, at all events, that her recent swoon must to a degree have enfeebled her mind, which would require time and the growth of spirits in her, and unstartled perception of the happiness that had come back from behind the veil, to recover its old tone.

"Agatha," he said, holding and caressing her hand, "you have passed through some strange experiences ; but it is well with us

both now, thanks be to Almighty God. Have
no fear. All that has happened is as natural
as sorrow is, or the shining of the sun, or the
darkness upon the earth when the night
comes. Your clear sense will presently see it
all."

She interrupted him. "Malcolm, the Verulam was burnt at sea, and I was placed in a
boat, the only woman in it—separated from my
father. The boat was steered by the boatswain of the ship, a man named Archer, who,
during our terrible sufferings, treated me with
noble goodness. We reached an island. This
man saved me from drowning; for the boat
was overset in the surf, and—and—where am
I *now?* Where is the island?" There was
again a look of consternation and amazement
in her wide open eyes.

"Do not you remember," he said, gently,
hoping to coax memory along in her, "that
I came to fetch you from the island in this
schooner, that I landed and found you and
Archer on the island, and brought you off to
this vessel, telling you that under God's guidance I had sought and found you, and that we
were going home, my beloved, going home to

dear old Wyloe, and to our friends there, and to our marriage?"

His hand trembled. He would have raised hers to his lips, but the bewilderment in her face arrested him and brought him back to his resolution of calmness and self-control.

"No, I do not remember. You say you found me on the island—strange!—I do not remember!"—and she frowned in her fierce struggle with thought.

"My darling," he said, still speaking very softly, guessing the truth, "tell me to what point does your memory carry you."

She took her hand from his, and leaned her temples upon her fingers, shutting her eyes. After a little she said slowly, and with intensity, "I remember three men on the island. One was Archer; he was very good to me. He made me a bed in a little cavern. He supplied me with food and water—such food as could be got—taking care that I should never want. I remember the dreadful loneliness of those days, the constant thunder of the surf that would sound like a roaring of wild beasts when the night was still. I remember feeling ill—so ill! and dreading

that I should die before help could come, and
that we should never meet again, Malcolm ;
though I had but small hope that we should
be rescued ; for I often heard the men talk
of the island being out of the track of ships
—I remember that." There was a pause ;,
she repeated, " Yes, I remember that. What
has happened since ?"

Down to this she had spoken with her eyes
closed, but when she asked the question she
let fall her hands and looked full at her lover.
For some moments he did not know what to
say. It was as plain to him by her manner as
was the silver splendour which lay upon the
skylight to his eyes, that the revivification of
her memory stopped short at her sufferings
upon the island, bringing her down may be,
though he dared not enquire *that* — to her
struggle with the seaman, and her swoon out
of which she awoke with her mind blinded.
All things this side, including that struggle,
were as dead to her as her previous past had
before been. He believed so, at least ; he
could not look at her and doubt it. The
mysterious mechanism of the mind had shifted
its burthen of darkness from one side of it to

the other. It was a marvellous thing for
him to witness in her, and he felt a
numbness coming out of it into his heart,
when, with the rapidity of thought, he considered that the recurrence of memory might
be but a passing, passionate effort of the
soul ere it lapsed into a blackness that
should stand as a lifelong eclipse of all
recollection in her.

Steadying his voice he said, ."My darling,
you have passed through so much, so much
that is heartbreaking even to think of, it is
not wonderful that memory in mercy should
hide from you a portion of the sufferings of
your shipwreck. Can you recall any circumstance associated with our passage, so far,
from the island?"

She answered, " I do not know where
I am."

" If I tell you," he exclaimed, "that this is
a little sailing vessel bearing you home to
Wyloe, can you understand me?"

" Oh, Malcolm, yes," she answered, with a
sweet smile.

" Do you recollect," he inquired, " a
French ship asking us if we would take

charge of a little baby that her people had picked up at sea?"

"No," she answered, with a strained expression in her eyes. There was a shadowing of tears, too, in the grey depths, with a hint of renewed terror growing.

He broke off in the sentence he had commenced, and cried out, "Agatha, dearest one—some things have happened which you cannot recall, but the true, the lovely, the sacred past is with you again, with you with all its love, and sunshine, and hopes. With you as I am, I who sought you and found you, though you knew me not, and for weeks have not known me, till this hour. It is enough for us, my precious one! God has answered my prayer. You know me—you remember me—you can pronounce my name——" He flung himself on his knees, grasping her round the waist, gazing up into her face with eyes of moving adoration; whilst she, putting her hands upon his head, pressed her lips to his forehead, and, speechless for many moments, they gazed at each other as though in a trance, amazement in her sleeping for awhile under the brooding emotion of joy, slowly perfecting itself with the perception of the reality of his beloved presence.

Hiram, peeping down the companion-way, saw them thus engrossed, and stepping on deck told Stone to keep clear of the cabin for the present, as though, for his part, he did not know much about love-making, he didn't need to be told that Fortescue and the lady were much too interested in the talk they had fallen into, to desire to be interrupted.

" Do she know him ?" asked Stone.

"Like one o'clock, Bill," responded Weeks. " Guv him his name slick out in a voice like singin'."

" I always said a little thing 'ud do it," said Stone. "A little thing he was, too. God receive him ! — as affectionate in his death as a holy angel, Hiram ; for take my word for it, 't was his love and gratitood for all she'd done for him as guv her back her memory."

The old man sent a wandering glance into the blue distance over the stern.

" Ye've made use of that fancy afore, Bill," exclaimed Hiram, " but I don't rightly follow it."

Stone looked hard over the side for a minute whilst he thought.

"Well," said he, "I allow it's one of them fancies as must catch hold of the onderstanding at once, because they're too delicate for explanation. There's a good many ideas as is best left alone if they don't make themselves intelligible right out of hand."

"Ay, that may be right enough," said Hiram, "but see here, Bill; I ain't a fool, matey; and if a fancy's plain to *you* I don't see why it shouldn't be plain to *me*."

Now, old Stone exactly understood the fancy that had seized him, but when he came to trying to express it he was at a loss. As he would afterwards say, ideas frequently occurred to him when he was lying in his bunk or drowsily standing his watch on a quiet night, which seemed to him full of beauty and poetry. They were in his mind, and he was able to think them out, yet he could no more have expressed them in words than he could have transformed the reflection of a star into the star itself. How could he make Hiram understand, having no language in which to shape his notion? His concep-

tion was that the devotion of Agatha had
been rewarded by the baby in his death;
for the coming back of her memory at the
moment of the child's burial was like a
sudden spiritualising of her, and God's
presence having been wondrously visible in
every passage of the schooner's mission, why
should not a miracle have been wrought
through the instrumentality of the bairn—a
miracle symbolising a woman's love, and
hope, and happiness, springing from the
ashes of the nameless babe she had taken
to her blinded heart and cherished? But
Stone could not explain. He felt indeed
that if he should attempt to do so he must
flounder, and perhaps destroy to himself the
fancy he was proud of and reckoned as
being highly poetical because it was his own.
So he got rid of the subject by asking
Weeks what Agatha had said when she
awoke from her faint, and this induced a chat
about the clergyman and Miss Fox, incidents
of the voyage, the time likely to be occupied
in reaching home, and so forth, which put
the men elbow to elbow, and set them
patrolling the deck with a sense of Sunday

strong upon them, owing to their being dressed in their best clothes, whilst the schooner, still off her course, pushed swiftly through the dark-blue waters with the shadows ever swaying like pendulums upon her deck, and in the shining hollows of her sails.

A long hour passed. Forward the men had finished their dinner, shifted into their old tarry rigs, and were at their various employments. The cook, with sulky eyes, frequently peered out of the galley, in the hope of intimating, by the expression on his countenance, that the cabin dinner was fast spoiling. Johnny came aft, and wanted to know if he should lay the cloth ; but had the lovers chosen to remain together for the rest of the day, Hiram would not have had them disturbed. At last Fortescue came on deck. He was pale, but there was a look of peace and quiet gladness in his face, which both Stone and Hiram instantly noticed. He approached them and said, " We have been selfish enough to occupy the cabin to your exclusion. I find it is long past the dinner hour."

"Oh, don't mention that, sir," said Hiram.

"Miss Fox is now lying down," continued the clergyman. "I doubt if any girl ever went through more than she has, physically and mentally."

"She has her memory, sir?" said Stone, respectfully.

"Ay, Mr. Stone, thank God she has her memory," exclaimed Fortescue. "It has returned to her perfect, down to the dreadful circumstance that caused her to lose it; of all that has happened since then she knows nothing."

"Nothing!" exclaimed Stone.

"*Nothing!*" repeated the clergyman, with solemn emphasis.

"Great thunder!" burst out Hiram, coming to a dead stand.

"Don't she remember our coming to her on the island, sir?" cried Stone.

"No."

"Nor the baby?" inquired Hiram, in a breathless way.

"It is wonderful! wonderful!" exclaimed Fortescue, clasping his hands, "yet it is so. She remembers *nothing* down to her swooning three hours ago. She has no recollection of the baby, nor of its burial, which has just taken place. It seems incredible. I stepped into her berth before she entered it to conceal all memorials of the poor little one—happily, Mr. Stone, you had already removed the crib —so that the light questions I put to her to test her memory of the baby, and of other incidents connected with the passage from the island, might not win a significance to frighten her by proofs of the things I spoke to her about. I will ask you, Captain Weeks, and you, Mr. Stone, to make no reference to the child, nor to anything which has happened since we left the island, in her presence. It is best that she should slowly realise that the memory which ought to cover the past few months is a blank. There is nothing to scare her in this nor to alarm me ; indeed, I would rather she should have the truth in my own version of it. It is, I take it, a special act of God's mercy that the horrible incident of her island life should be hidden to her for ever, and as a thing likely to keep her heart sad it is as well, perhaps, Mr. Stone," looking at the old man with an emotion almost of affection

kindling in his fine dark eyes, "that the
memory of our poor little baby should be
sealed from her."

Both Stone and Hiram knuckled their
foreheads in recognition of the clergyman's
wishes, and then Stone said, "If she has
her memory perfect down to the point you
name, what more could she need, sir, pro-
widing, of course, that she goes on afresh
from this morning without any more stop-
pages ?"

"There's only this," said Hiram, with a
nervous look aloft and a hesitating glance
around, "if Miss Fox has got no memory
of this here woyage, she'll never be able to
appreciate the way we made the island she
was cast upon, nor the sailing of the Golden
Hope, and her behaviour in all sorts of
weather."

"Oh, but she will," said Fortescue, smiling.
"Her present memory will enable her to
preserve the recollection of what I tell her
touching the voyage, and that being so,
Captain Weeks, it will be *my* fault if she
doesn't fully appreciate the beauty of this
little vessel, your skill as a navigator, and

the loyalty and high qualities of our great-hearted old friend here," and he laid his hand upon Stone's shoulder.

"Well, sir," said Stone, looking as though this condescending act of Mr. Fortescue would break him down, "I can only say from the bottom of my soul I'm glad—I'm glad things have turned out as they have. I always felt as that a little thing 'ud do it."

"Stone thinks the baby did it, Mr. Fortescue," said Hiram.

"The lady's memory," observed Stone, looking down upon the deck, "a-coming back to her at the moment when the little hammock flashed off the plank into the water, seemed to me as if it was the gratitood of the h'infant for Miss Fox's cherishing of him that did it. Hiram here don't understand," continued the old man, with a glance at the skipper, "but that ain't my fault."

"*I* understand," said Mr. Fortescue, thoughtfully, and obviously impressed by the rough sailor's fancy.

"Well, it's beyond my larning," exclaimed Hiram, slightly vexed, apparently, by the clergyman's ready apprehension of Stone's

notion, "but a ship's fo'ksle ain't much of
a college, and so there's no call for me to
'pologise. Here you, Johnny!" he bawled,
"bear a hand now with the cabin dinner.
How's her head, Jim?"

The course was given.

"Ha!" exclaimed Hiram. "So she's come
up to it? Bill," said he, turning to Stone,
"if the trades ain't humming in our rigging
to-night you shall call me a farmer, and
watch me pick the hayseeds out o' my
hair."

When dinner was served, Fortescue stole
softly to Agatha's door to ascertain if she
was awake. Not hearing her, he noiselessly
peeped in, and observed her in deep sleep.
If ever love is stirred in the fond heart of
a man it is when he leans over his beloved,
watching her face in slumber. Whatever of
sweetness or loveliness there is, whatever of
gentleness of expression, of womanly purity
of lineament, is chastened into deeper elo-
quence of aspect by the serenity of sleep.
Agatha lay in her bunk, with her cheek rest-
ing on her hand, her face towards the cabin
door; the high sunshine flowed in sparkling

gushings through bull's-eye and scuttle, but so slenderly, owing to the smallness of the points of admission, as to mellow rather than illuminate the atmosphere of the berth, so that just such a light rested upon the girl as the enchanting simplicity of her beauty would show the most tenderly in. The clergyman stayed a little while to gaze upon her. She was his own now, such as she had not been since she had started from him when he found her in her leafy home on the island, and the joy of this knowledge made love and gratitude fervent in him beyond words; for he need dread no longer her perpetual blindness to that past in which their affection had its growth; he need no longer half-despairingly dream of rearing upon the blackened caverns of her memory another love, whose roots would have but such soil to feed on as her new existence should be able to thinly scatter over them; he need no longer dread the withering up of her fair and fruitful intellect by the deadly blight of melancholy. She lay before him, his Agatha of Wyloe, his heart's delight, his first and only and enduring love; beautiful in her sleep with a smile of rest upon her lips. Then indeed, with a force of realization he had never before reached to, chilled and checked as he had been by her unrecognising eyes, by her growing despondency and frosty insensibility ; *then* his mind compassed the whole significance of his voyage ; the desolation and misery God had sent him to rescue her from ; the glorious privilege conferred upon him by his Maker, of finding upon, and delivering from, a tiny rock upon the boundless immensity of the ocean, the one in all this world who was so dear to him that the greatness of his emotion rebuked in his own heart every effort to give it utterance, as unworthy of the truth.

He left her sleeping, and seated himself with the two plain seamen, both of whom took care to tell him that sleep was the best thing for her, that the brain found energy in repose, and so forth ; and they conversed with such a strenuous effort of whisper that they purpled their faces with their singular attempts to make little more than inarticulate hoarseness stand for sympathetic opinion and solid advice.

Anyway, good care was taken that the most delicate meal the schooner could provide should be ready for Agatha when she awoke, which happened five hours after she had withdrawn to her berth. With sleep-flushed beauty she came timidly from her berth, pausing in the doorway with spangles on every loose hair that fluffed above her head, caught from the westering, crimson lustre upon the skylight, and resembling particles of gold-dust floating over her. Her lover, who had been thrice to her berth to assure himself that she still slept and that all was well, sat, as he had sat for an hour, at the cabin table, patient and often listening, with a book before him. She cried out, "Malcolm, my darling! My darling! My dreams have been all about you."

He took her in his arms and brought her to the table, scanning with deepest love her features, and striving, as you would have said, to pierce to her very soul through the soft grey light of her eyes. How great was the change! It was all the difference between the statue of marble and the same peerless shape warmed into flesh and blood,

and spiritualised! The unheeding, sorrowful
look of the eyes, bitterly wistful when gazing
away into distance, was gone; the radiance
of memory was in them; the full illumination
of perfect intelligence was upon her face.
Marvellous transformation! Could it be,
indeed, as poor, unlettered old Stone had
suggested, that it was the little baby's gift of
love; that, as a tiny bairn, being nearer than
all mortal things of older growth to the
angels, the mite had been chosen as a
messenger, and called back to Heaven, having
worked out the end he had been sent to
fulfil? It was a fancy that at this moment
fired Fortescue's superstitious mind, and his
brain was full of it as he held the girl to him,
searching her face.

Her long sleep had greatly refreshed her,
and completely steadied her mind. She could
not remove her eyes from her lover. There
was a perpetual surprise of joy in her gaze,
and whilst she sat at the meal that he had
provided for her, she would not let him leave
her side; and often she slipped her hand into
his, looking up at him with a happiness full of
wonder. During the while they had been to-

gether in the cabin, before she withdrew to
her berth to sleep, he had taken care to test
her memory by the lightest references only to
the past, more particularly to his voyage in
search of her. Her condition had demanded
this precaution, because, although her memory
was active enough to satisfy him that the
faculty was intact, saving its blindness to
the things of the past few weeks, yet there
had been a certain vagueness, a kind of confusion in her way of looking back and thinking and talking of such recollections as he
carefully and softly invited her to. Nor
indeed could he be sure that, though the
power of recalling the past had come to her,
it would remain, seeing how a long span, dat-
ing from the day of her discovery upon the
island down to that morning, was as dead to
her as though the events included in it had
been dreamt of by him alone, and were without reality. But now as he conversed, he
observed how sleep had sharpened and in-
vigorated her faculties ; and this encouraging
him, he told her by degrees, with many a
loving look between them, and pauses for
emotion, how it had come about that he had

sought her on that tiny island, whereon she had been cast by shipwreck.

He related how he had stood upon Deal beach watching the Indiaman gliding under the stars, and vanishing round the Foreland, with the meteor breaking and expiring over her mastheads ; how in his sleep he had beheld the full picture of the burning of the Verulam ; the open boat in which she sat with Archer at her side, and dead men lolling over the bows, and figures languishing and death-stricken upon the thwarts ; how he had witnessed the upsetting of the boat in the surf, her rescue by Archer, her thanksgiving for her deliverance, her appeal to him with outstretched arms to come to her.

The tears sprang into her eyes when he came to this part. She murmured, " I remember ! I remember ! It was a wild, strange, perhaps mad hope in me, Malcolm, that by stretching out my arms to you, where I could behold you in imagination, you might see me, too, and know my condition, and come to me. What was in my mind I can recollect. Some story you once told me, darling, showing the power love gives to the heart, of making its thoughts known to another, though widely sundered as the ends of the world."

A little colour entered her cheeks, and she hung her head to say under her breath, "That was the fancy in my mind, Malcolm, even at such a moment."

He pressed her hand and went on to relate how, after he had dreamt of her, he had awakened and found in his room a drawing of the island he had beheld in his sleep; how, one day, news came of the destruction of the Verulam, every particular of which, as he afterwards discovered, exactly tallied with the details of his vision; how this had satisfied him that the information of his dream was a direct whisper from a merciful and loving God. He spoke of his offer of a reward to anyone who should tell him where the island was; he told how the little drawing he had circulated had fallen into Stone's hands and brought the old seaman to call upon him at Wyloe, and how, acting under Stone's advice, he had purchased the schooner and sailed to the Indian Ocean to seek her. She listened at times breathlessly. A look of awe, that made her beauty indescribable, came upon her when he mentioned his vision, and how he had drawn a sketch of the island in his sleep with such accuracy that Stone, who had been wrecked there, instantly recognised it. In this, as in other incidents he mentioned, she could witness now, as he had witnessed all along, the near, actual presence and inter-position of the Most High. He felt her tremble; she leaned her head as if in worship. To her pure and righteous mind her lover's narrative gave indeed a sanctity to the very atmosphere about them. It was as if they had been chosen agents for a miracle de-signed to exhibit Heaven's shaping and con-trolling power, by an illustration outside the familiar discipline of the universe, and not without correspondence with the old wonder-ful workings of the Unseen Hand.

As both Weeks and Stone took particular care not to intrude upon them, the time slipped insensibly away over their long con-versation, their scores of questions, their fre-quent caresses and prayerful pauses; for indeed this was their first meeting, heart to heart, soul to soul, since he had bade her farewell on board the Verulam ; and there were a thousand things to speak and ask about, and to recall. Until in due course the cabin glooming rapidly to the quick twilight of those parts, Fortescue started and looked at his watch.

"Let us go on deck," he exclaimed. "We have been nearly the whole day below."

He fetched her hat for her, for it was observable that she was now at fault in things which had grown familiar to her during the passage from the island. It was his sealskin cap, for she had Stone's big hat on the other side of the Cape, and had been wearing the warmer head-gear through and along the chilly parallels. She took it, looked at it with a smile, and put it on her head with the most womanly, natural glance in the world at the strip of glass fixed against the bulkhead. On their emerging she came to a stand at the hatch, with one hand upon the companion or hood of it, glancing up and then forward with eager, inquiring eyes, the expression in which was visible enough to the clergyman, for the sunset yet lay in a dusky blush low down over the sea-line.

"And this," she exclaimed, in a low voice,
"is the vessel that came to us to the island—
the vessel you bought to rescue me with?"
She seized his hand, holding it tightly.

It was wonderful to hear her, shocking indeed, for the space of a breath to Fortescue.
There had been a dreadful mental mystery to
him in the gaze of her eyes turned upon him
without recognition, but yet when the first
crushing effects of it upon him had been
eased by time, and he had thought closely
over it, he had ceased to find anything violent
in the phenomenon she submitted of an intellect operating with apparent healthfulness and
clearness, whilst shorn of one of the essential
principles of reason.   But her not knowing
the schooner after the long weeks she had
spent on board, her standing at the hatch
and looking around her, and speaking of the
vessel as something she was now beholding
for the first time, staggered and dumb-
founded him.   It was certain that the
memory she had brought with her from the
island was artificial, without any depth, and
that its going was like the evanishment of
a bubble, that in bursting wastes upon the

colourless air the hundred gleaming pictures
its irridiscent texture had reflected.

He rallied promptly, and putting her arm
under his, led her to Stone and Weeks.

" This," he said, looking at the mate, " is
Mr. Stone, who brought me a description of
the island and its whereabouts. Without
him I should not have been able to save
you."

She took the old fellow's hand ; he pulled
off his cap, bowing himself respectfully whilst
she spoke.

" I thank you for my life, Mr. Stone,"
she said. " Mr. Fortescue has told me a
wonderful story. You happening to know
the island he saw in his dream is not the
least marvellous part of it."

" And this," said Mr. Fortescue, " is
Captain Weeks, to whose skilful navigation
we are indebted for our speedy recovery
of you."

Hiram flourished his cap as if he were
signalling a distant ship ; but, like Stone,
he made no reply, for the simple reason
that, like Stone, he was taken unawares
and had nothing ready.

Since she had not known the schooner, it was impossible to suppose that she recognised Stone and the captain ; but this could not be known because the clergyman's action had been an introduction of her, so to speak, and under the circumstances she would have addressed them in the same way whether she remembered them or not. She asked for Archer. Stone went forward, and in a minute or two Archer came along the deck. It was now very nearly dark. She looked close into his face to see, and then instantly recognising him, brought her hands together in a quick passionate clasp, and cried, "Oh! Mr. Archer, 'tis good of God to have led my love into the solitude of the ocean to save us. That you should have been preserved — you, whose goodness to me, whose care for me in the boat was that of an Englishman of noble heart— you who protected me on the island, obtained food for me, found me a shelter, watched over me——" She broke off, and then vehemently turning to Fortescue she exclaimed, "Oh, Malcolm, the saving of this man, this brave and generous seaman, makes my deliverance doubly sweet to me!"

"And to me," said Mr. Fortescue.

Cap in hand, standing erect, Archer said, "I did but what was right, miss. I thank you for your good words. I shall treasure your praise."

The girl remaining silent, the clergyman found she was crying. He said, "My darling, I must not let you overtax yourself. It has been a day full of wonder and happiness for us both." He leaned aside towards Archer and whispered, "She has her memory, dear friend. All of her past she remembers to—to the hour in that dreadful night. This passage, from the island down to to-day is an utter blank. Let it be so."

"Right, sir," answered Archer, in the same swift whisper in which Fortescue had addressed him, "and I say thank God she knows ye, for I onderstand what that must mean for both you and her." He pulled a lock of hair and walked forward.

The breeze had fallen with the sinking of the sun. The schooner, with fanning canvas, glided quietly along a sea that was like the English Channel on a summer night for the smoothness of it, and the air was full of a

dim, soft, golden haze of starlight.   Agatha,
drinking in the pleasant atmosphere, hung
with hands locked upon her lover's arm,
slowly walking the length of the quarter-
deck with him.   There was little else to
disturb the stillness but the low humming of
their speech.   At the tiller stood Goldsmith,
a dark and quiet shape.   Stone leaned
against the bulwark, withdrawing himself
into shadow and obscurity, as it might have
seemed as though from eager anxiety not to
even suggest the obtrusion of his personality
upon the lovers.   Forward in the darkness
upon the forecastle the glowing bowl of a
pipe or two might have been detected ; but
all was silent that way.   The memory of the
babe was yet fresh, and now that the darkness had come, the death of the nameless
infant and its burial were felt again in the
forecastle.

But a little before half-past eight, down
in the south-east quarter, you would have
observed a shadow blackening upon the sea,
and rising with it, here and there, a cloud,
pale against the stars,   In a short time the
new wind was blowing between the masts of

the schooner, and the watch on deck filled the scene between the bulwarks with busy flittings and dartings as they tumbled about, hauling and pulling.

" The first of the south-east trade, I do believe," cried out old Stone to Hiram, as the captain came probing his long body through the companion-way. The old man was right, as was Hiram, who had predicted it ; for long before midnight the schooner, under fore-topmast stunsail and swelling squaresail, was rushing through the seas before a noble wind blowing strong over the quarter, with a heaven of stars leaping among driving clouds, and the foam whitening out spectrally in all directions like snow-drifts upon a giant moor, steeped in the shadow of night and vast in the darkness.

CHAPTER THE LAST.

HOME.

IT is autumn in England. Past the fringe of trees which about define the limits of Wyloe in the west, the sun is setting with a fiery wild light that has a tempestuous appearance, because of the swirling and boiling aspect of the scarlet, glowing haze which trembles a blood-like ardency through the boughs, and floats far into the east over the delicate greenish azure of the sky. Where the sea stretches westward the water is as scarlet as the heaven. The shingle heaves towards the surf along its margin in billows which resemble surges arrested in their career; every stone and pebble have upon them the rich purple of the expiring light, and so deep is the country silence that even in the heart of Wyloe you may plainly hear the washing of the froth running with a delicate seething sound through the air, the peculiar note of which is distinct above the murmur of the voices around, or even the coarse jolting rattle of some cart on the high-way beyond. The eastward-facing walls of the old church stand black in the long dark shadow of the building, and cast an early night upon the graves there, but the weather-cock on the tower has the glowing sunshine still upon it, and streaks the sky like a beam of deep red light. You could tell, without inquiring, that there is a sense of expectation in Wyloe this evening. It may be detected in such minute signs as the head or two which will pop out of open windows or shop doors at intervals, always glancing up the street towards the " Barley Mow " inn, where the coach stops that comes from Dover. It is also noticeable when old people chance to meet ; a shambling couple, say, who as men and women would be content at any other time to call a greeting to each other in their cracked and feeble pipes as they passed, for the excellent reason that their minds hold nothing to warrant a dead stop, that is, nothing outside their half-score of threadbare local topics, which to deal with according to custom they would need an armchair, a pipe, a cup of tea, or any such excuse. But this evening they come to a halt. Garrulity is strong in the noses which they thrust into each other's face. They strike the pavement with their sticks, and pretend to turn away as if they indeed meant to part, but their noses come together again, and so for half an hour at a time.

At the Vicarage the dining-room windows are open, for the air is soft and pleasant. A lamp stands upon the table, lighted candles upon the mantelpiece. A goat bleats tremulously somewhere out in the dusk. There are four people in this room. One is the Reverend Alfred Clayton, Vicar of Wyloe; the other is his brother, Doctor Joseph Clayton; the third and fourth are Mrs. Clayton and her daughter Josephine. The ladies are seated, the gentlemen are pacing the carpet, like sentries, only the doctor is much more active than the parson, who fills the apartment with a sound of wheezing as he goes. In the doctor, indeed, it is a kind of flitting, but the movements of both are full of nervousness and agitation, and presently Mrs. Clayton finds this activity rather irritating.

"My dear," she says, addressing the Vicar, "I wish you would sit down. I dare say if you were to feel my pulse you would find that my heart beats faster than yours, which would prove, of course, that my excitement is greater than yours."

"Not necessarily," interrupted the doctor.

"Yet," continued Mrs. Clayton, "I can repress my feelings and behave, at all events, as if I were composed."

"I can't sit down," said Mr. Clayton.

"Nor I," exclaimed the doctor.

"Only consider," the Vicar continued, coming to a stand opposite his wife, and talking asthmatically, "for months and months we have been in ignorance of our dear Agatha's fate. For months and months we have been convinced that Fortescue is the victim of a distressing delusion, and that he is voyaging on a quest merely to perish by the way or return with a heart broken by disappointment. Instead of which, only yesterday morning I get a letter from

him saying that he is alive, that he has
Agatha with him, that they are both well,
that they have arrived off Deal in the
Golden Hope, that they are lingering to
make some purchases at Deal, and expect
to be here this evening at seven o'clock."
He pulled out his watch. " How can I sit
down?" he added.   " Excitement ! why, here
is a miracle—a miracle."

" I only mean," said Mrs. Clayton, "that
it increases one's own nervousness when
other people are restless."

" Hush !" cried the doctor, hollowing his
hands round his ear at the window, and
thrusting his head out.   .

After a little, asthma conquered, and the
Rev. Alfred Clayton sat down.

The doctor was naturally of a dark complexion, with the Indian's dusky eye, but he
now showed himself burnt to the colour of
ground coffee. Indeed, had he acted as a
ship's figure-head in a voyage round the
world, his skin could hardly have been more
unsparingly tanned.

" Curse the moths !" he suddenly cried, as
a great fellow, big as a butterfly, sailed in

through the window, and went slapping
about the ceiling with a noise like the toeing
of a sailor in a jig. "We shan't be able to
hear anything for that creature's wings."

" The more one thinks of it," exclaimed
the Vicar, "the more absolutely incredible
and marvellous it seems. A man is in love
with a girl. She sails for India ; the ship is
burnt, and the people take to the boats. The
lover dreams of the loss of the ship, sees an
island in a vision with his sweetheart upon it,
finds out where the island is, sells a couple of
thousand pounds worth of securities, buys a
little ship, and steers for this spot of land
somewhere in the Indian Ocean. Why," he
exclaimed, "it must be, since he has her
with him, that he found her on the island,
and that every circumstance of the voyage
corroborated his dream."

" It is a great pity," says Josephine, "that
Mr. Fortescue should not have said so in his
letter. To be kept all this time wondering !
If he really found her on the island the whole
thing will be almost too awful."

" Why ?" asked Mrs. Clayton.

" Well, if it happened to me, I mean if I

were to dream as Mr. Fortescue did, and it came true, it would make me feel as if I was unnatural and belonged to the period of the Old Testament, and had been selected."

"He says Agatha is well," says Dr. Clayton, "but how about that lung of hers, I wonder. This and her general health had greatly improved even before we got to the Cape ; of that there is no doubt."

"Dear me," said Mrs. Clayton, with a nervous twitch in her chair. "I wish they would come."

But they had to wait, and then Dr. Clayton, bringing his head from the window and crying out, "I hear the coach!" ran without his hat out of the house, leaving the others moving about the room in the last stage of restlessness, anxiety and consuming expectation.

Another ten minutes ; the sound of eager voices outside. Mrs. Clayton and Josephine run into the hall, the Vicar goes puffing after them ; the door is wide open ; the figure of a girl bounds up the steps, and in a breath the hall is full of people, kissing, crying, shaking hands and the like. Nor does this complete the picture, for there are some scores of parishioners who had got to hear that their curate was coming back with the shipwrecked sweetheart he had gone in search of, and who, on seeing Mr. Fortescue and Agatha alight from the coach, followed them and the doctor into the Vicarage grounds, where they stood like a wall, waiting until the embracing was over in the hall to cheer. The opportunity arrived; a perfect yell of welcome like a hurricane swept out of those hearty seaside lungs of leather; the shout is again repeated, and no one could have imagined for how long a time these excellent people would have stayed, if the Vicar had not stood upon the step, thanked them in the name of his curate and the lady for their cordial reception, told them that Mr. Fortescue was too much affected to address even a sentence to them, and so dismissed them.

Half an hour later there was something like composure among the inmates of the Vicarage, but until then there had been little more than explanations, touching illustrations of Agatha's delight in finding her step-father alive and well, questions from the Vicar diverted from their purpose by Mrs. Clayton, who declared that she would not have Agatha and Mr. Fortescue worried until they had supped and were rested, and fully capable of stating their adventures. But human nature could not stand out. There was a limit, and it was arrived at shortly after they had seated themselves at the cheerful, abundant supper-table.

"Only one question, Fortescue," rapped out the Vicar, "nothing further, I give you my word, until after supper—but—but—*did* you find Agatha on the island ?"

"Yes," responded Fortescue.

The Reverend Mr. Clayton rolled up his eyes to the ceiling. Josephine clasped her hands and looked thrilled. The doctor uttered, "Amazing! Amazing!" and Mrs. Clayton said, addressing her husband, "Do please go on carving, my dear."

However, before the supper was over the doctor had told his story, at all events. He had made one of forty people in the long-boat of the Verulam. It was not until the dawn broke that he found he was separated from his step-daughter; for though the flames burnt fiercely in the fore part of the Verulam, it was impossible for him even by their light to distinguish the faces of the crowd which brought the boat low in the water. Their sufferings, however, did not last long, for on the evening of the second day they were sighted by a French brig bound to Mauritius, that bore down and took them on board, where, indeed, owing to the numerous crew of Frenchmen and the smallness of the vessel's accommodation, they were not very much better off than they had been in the long-boat. Five days after, an Indiaman belonging to the firm that owned the Verulam over hauled the brig, and the captain on hearing who were the people the Frenchman had picked up, immediately consented to receive the whole of them. In this manner the doctor made his way to England, but very much against his wishes, forhis destination had been Bombay, and he naturally concluded that if the people in the boat in which Agatha was, were rescued, there was much more likelihood of their being conveyed to some adjacent port, whence Agatha would be able to make her way to Bombay, than carried to England. But it could not be helped. The little doctor was brought to

London, and from there proceeded to Wyloe, at which place, on hearing from his brother of Fortescue's extraordinary dream, and the singular quest he had embarked on, he determined to remain until news of Agatha or Fortescue should reach him.

Such was the doctor's story; but he related every particular, was excessively minute, and made much of the loss of his luggage and some valuable books in the Verulam, and of his sufferings in the boat, and on the French brig, so that, frequently interrupted as he was by questions, the termination of his narrative found the supper-cloth removed, and the Claytons, who had heard the doctor's story over and over again, all throbbing with anxiety for Fortescue to begin.

And yet, though in the curate's own mind what he had undergone might have appeared to him to warrant the furnishing out of a sitting that should last for days, when it came to his talking he found that there was but little to say. He gave them the story, plainly related one or two incidents of the passage to the island, his misgivings touching Stone's accuracy, Hiram's doubts, the fears which would haunt him that after all the vision that had impelled him might prove as delusive as dreams usually are ; his anxiety as the hour for the island to heave in view approached, the profound conviction which seized him that the finger of Almighty God had pointed the way, when the land stood fair before him in the calm waters, a conformation startling by familiarity, since he knew it as a man might know any place he had visited. He told them about his landing, how he had found Agatha ; but now a conspicuous reserve marked his narrative. He simply let them suppose that on finding Agatha he led her to the boat. Nothing was said about her loss of memory.

Meanwhile, she sat listening to him, with eyes that seemed to adore him, rooted to his face. He was silent on the subject of the baby.

"The Golden Hope," he said, "is a wonderful sailer, and our run from the Line to the English Channel showed an average of two hundred miles a day. We anchored off Deal, and I induced Agatha to remain on board whilst I went ashore in search of someone qualified to make her fit to travel in a stage-

coach." He laughed, running his eyes over
her dress and taking up her hand and kissing
it.

" How on earth, Agatha dear," exclaimed
Miss Clayton, "did you manage on that
island ?"

" My bedroom was a cave," she answered.

" I understood you to say that the men built
her a summer-house, Fortescue," broke in the
doctor.

" Agatha slept in a cave," said Fortescue,
giving the doctor a peculiar look.

" How long were you on the island ? " asked
the Vicar.

Agatha thought, glanced wistfully at her
lover, and then looked on the floor with a
slightly troubled expression, which the doctor's
keen eye noticed.

" No matter, my dearest," said he. " I am
grateful to God to find you looking so well.
Your eyes are amazingly bright and clear ;
your complexion is also as it should be." He
put his thumb upon her wrist. " All's well
that ends well, my love," said he, soothingly.
" I will sound your lung to-morrow, but I
expect to find it perfectly healthy."

"Were the sailors kind on the island?" said Mrs. Clayton.

This started the girl, for memory could help her here. She told them about her sufferings in the boat, about Archer's noble humanity and goodness to her, how the boat went to pieces in the surf, and how Archer rescued her. She also told them about her island life, the food they had managed to get, the warm fresh-water springs they had found, and so forth, but they all noticed the abrupt pause in her relation when, whilst it was obvious to them that only half of the time she had been upon the island was accounted for by the incidents she narrated, she stopped as if the story ended there. The impression was that there was a something behind, which both she and Fortescue desired to conceal, because his reserve in its way had not been less suggestive than her making out that her life on the island had come to an end, when, in reality, she must have passed many more weeks upon it ere the arrival of the schooner.

The doctor looked worried; yet for an hour longer they went on talking, one question leading to another till you would have supposed there was nothing more to tell. Then Agatha owned she was wearied, and would be glad to go to bed, on which the bell rung, servants arrived, and after the usual prayers were read, the Vicar knelt and offered up thanksgiving to God for the preservation of the life of Agatha, for His guidance of Fortescue, for their happy return. Much more he said, deeply affected himself, and using such tender, moving language, that there was a frequent sound of sobbing heard whilst he prayed.

The ladies then withdrew, and the little doctor looked about him for his pipe.

"Where are you going?" said the Vicar to Fortescue.

"To seek a bed," said he, laughing. "I will run round to my old lodging whilst the people are still awake."

"No, no; a room is ready for you here. Sit down, my dear friend. How bronzed you are! Almost as black as my brother. The sea is a brave life. I sometimes wish I'd been a sailor."

"Yes, a brave life to look at through a window," said Fortescue, smiling.

"Sit down, Fortescue," said the doctor; "here is a pouch of excellent tobacco. I want you to tell me about Agatha. Something ails her mentally. Is it her memory?" He fixed his black eyes, full of anxious scrutiny, upon the curate.

"It is," answered Fortescue, "but, thank God, it is not as it was when I found her. Ah!" he exclaimed, covering his face with his hands, and speaking in that posture, "what I have endured, what I have suffered on the grounds of her memory only, can never be known, save to my Maker!"

He lingered so long with his face hidden that they supposed him to be in prayer, and neither of them spoke. After a little he looked up, and then in a broken way at first, but gaining ground as he proceeded, he told them how, when he had first come across Agatha on the island, he had seen her lying wildly beautiful in her tattered raiment upon the ground of the little house of boughs, striving to collect in the palm of her hand a pool of sunshine beside her; she had looked at him in a half-witted manner, as he deemed, and with absolutely unrecognising eyes, and

then he found her memory was gone, that she
knew him not, had not the faintest knowledge
of her past. This was confirmed by the brave
fellow Archer, who afterwards narrated in the
cabin of the schooner in what dreadful manner it had come about that recollection was
destroyed in her. The whole story he told
them ; of the baby who had been put aboard
by the French man-of-war; of the girl's extraordinary devotion and love for the little one ;
of its falling from her arms into the sea ;
her anguish ; the babe's burial ; the miracu-
lous restoration of Agatha's memory at that
moment; the equally marvellous benumbment,
or utter extinction, of her capacity of recalling
a single circumstance from the time previous
to her struggle with the seaman down to her
awakening from the swoon that followed her
recognition of her lover.

They listened with amazement, more particularly the Vicar, who looked as if he was
now certain that the age of miracles had
returned. Dr. Clayton, puffing at his pipe,
said, " Is her memory, as regards the
interval you speak of, still dead?"

" Yes. Once, very cautiously, about a fort-

night ago, I touched upon the subject of the
baby, wondering whether such a reference to
emotions so vital as those the poor little infant had excited in her, would stir her recollection. It did not ; she gazed at me blankly."

" To think," cried the Vicar, clasping his
hands, "that out of the death of a little child,
the memory, the happiness of one who
loved it should come back to her ! What
wondrous justification of the truth and
beauty of that saying of our Lord, ' Whosoever shall receive one of these children in My
name, receiveth Me, and whosoever shall
receive Me, receiveth not Me, but Him that
sent Me.' You took that infant in God's
name, and the Spirit of God came to you
with it and blessed you both."

" Yes. I felt that over and over again,"
said Fortescue.

" But her memory, as regards her past,
down to the moment when you say recollection ceases, is perfect ?" inquired the
doctor.

" As perfect as ever it was," answered the
curate.

" All things," continued the doctor, " which

have happened since her recognition of you she can recollect?"

"Yes—all things. You may liken her memory to a chain. A dark shadow lies upon a few links. The rest is in sunshine."

"It may be the design of Heaven," said the Vicar, "that she should not recollect the dreadful thing that befel her upon the island."

"Ay," exclaimed Fortescue, "and I believe it was Heaven's will that her memory should leave her, that health of body might return. The past was struck out. Her mind could catch hold of nothing to fret over. When I found her she resembled some ocean goddess, a soft tropical glow in her cheeks, an exquisite dancing freedom in her movement, as careless as the breeze and as radiant. There was a far richer health in her beauty than is now visible, for she fretted inwardly when she came to know from me that she had a memory to which she was blind, and that I who stood before her was her lover, betrothed to her, but unknown to her."

Dr. Clayton rose and paced the room. He delivered a long medical opinion upon the singular mental problem that Agatha had,

and in a great degree still, submitted. He
said that the recovery of her health through
the loss of her memory was in its way as
wonderful as any other feature of the voyage
and rescue; yet so conceivable that no
student of psychology could question the
accuracy of the theory that attributed recovery to a loss of all recollection of whatever could keep her fretting and despairful.

He declared himself on the whole as not
uneasy on the score of the second lapse of
memory, and said that in all probability it
was for the best that she should not be able
to recall the assault that had shocked memory
out of her—at least until her mind had re-
gained the old vigour. He added he did not
doubt that in time recollection would fill the
hiatus; and having thus delivered himself, he
spoke of other marvels of this strange passage
in two human lives, more particularly Fortescue's vision, and then the conversation went
over the whole ground of the voyage again.

. . . .

As darkness deepens into midnight over
Wyloe, and the extinguished lights in the
Vicarage leave the house a black shadow

among the trees which surround it, the
writer pauses, finding his story told.   For
the curate's quest is over ; he has brought
his beloved back in safety and in health ;
and it was but to relate the voyage that this
narrative was entered upon.   There are, indeed, other scenes beyond.   The return of
the curate to his old life and habits, glimpses
of Agatha, sweet and gentle, winning love
on all hands, narrating again and again the
story of her shipwreck and of her life upon
the island so far as memory carried her ;
Doctor Clayton's discovery, confirmed by the
London physician who had advised the voyage, that her lung was perfectly sound ; her
marriage to Fortescue in the December
following their arrival, and the return of the
doctor to India a month later.

Out of all these things another volume
could be made, but the story is long enough.
Yet the Golden Hope ! That brave schooner
which carried the clergyman to the island of
his dream ! What of her ? And of William
Stone and Hiram Weeks, and old William
Breeches and the rest of that little company
of souls ?

Well, first of the Golden Hope, and then a sentence or two for the men, ere they are dismissed into that shadowy land out of which the pen of the novelist summoned them. On the arrival of the schooner at the East India Docks, Fortescue wrote to his relative, Mr. Salt, to ask him to negotiate the sale of her. He had no further need of her, he said ; she had enabled him to accomplish his mission ; when he thought of her it was as of a living being, lovely, loyal, and affectionate, and were he a richer man he would not part with her for four times the sum she cost him. But he was now about to incur many expenses, and it was out of the question that he could preserve the vessel merely as a relic. On the top of this letter Mr. Salt came down to Wyloe, was very handsomely received by the Vicar, introduced to Agatha, with whom he fell in love, and now hearing from Fortescue the motives and causes which led to his undertaking the voyage, for as we know the clergyman had concealed from his relative all about his dream and its startling corroboration, he was so much impressed with the story that he declared the schooner ought to be kept in the family; and, declining to listen to Fortescue's entreaties that he would take time to consider the matter, he wrote him a cheque that included not only the price the Golden Hope had cost the curate, but all the expenses of her provisioning, wages and the like, along with the one hundred guineas that was to be Stone's reward for determining the position of the island.   For four years the old gentleman used the Golden Hope as a yacht, and talked so much of the marvellous errand his relative had put her upon, that people looked at her as if she was a curiosity, the remains of something sacred and full of mystery.   Mr. Salt, then finding himself growing too old for yachting, sold her for a few hundred pounds to a man who started her afresh in her old business of carrying cargoes of fruit.   Six months after this, news reached Fortescue that the Golden Hope had been in collision in the Bay of Biscay and foundered with the loss of two of her crew.

William Stone not only received the hundred guineas, but a very handsome gift of money besides, subscribed to by Dr. Clayton; Wrotham, Skinner and Co.—who were greatly pleased with the conduct of their old servant—Mr. Salt and Fortescue. Archer also met with the liberal treatment the poor fellow nobly deserved. Nor was Hiram forgotten. He was made happy by a gift of fifty pounds and a very fine telescope ; the inscription on which was complimentary enough to keep the old fellow smiling every time he had occasion to use the glass. Every one of the crew, from old Bill Breeches down to Johnny, the boy, received, according to his rating, a substantial gift of money over and above his wages, so that even the surly and superstitious cook had to admit that, now the astonishing voyage was over, he had every reason to be satisfied that he had signed articles for the Golden Hope.

But Jack is a fugitive creature. Of the three principal seamen concerned in this tale the first to entirely disappear was Archer. He stayed ashore for some time, giving out that he had had enough of the sea, and meant to "knock off" and start in a little business, now that he had a trifle of money to call his own. He went down to Wyloe two or three times, where he was received as a greatly-prized friend, and talked to Fortescue about the sort of business he might consider himself best qualified for, and was evidently in earnest. Some time went by, and Fortescue not hearing of him, wrote to learn how he was getting on, when to the great grief of Agatha and himself, there came back a letter from Mrs. Archer saying that her husband, having grown uneasy at the idea of remaining ashore, had determined to make one more voyage. He had found a berth as boatswain on board a vessel bound to the West Indies. She had shifted her cargo in the English Channel during heavy weather, and Archer entering the hold to lend the men a hand to trim the stuff that was tumbling about, had been so cruelly crushed that he died shortly after he had been sent ashore.

The next to fade out was Hiram. Fortescue was never able to learn what his end was, or what had become of him, supposing he still lived.

Old William Stone lingered long—long enough to dance three of Agatha's babies upon his knee, to cut out and rig little boats for the eldest of them when he was in his fifth year, to spin long yarns at Fortescue's table, to divert and even to charm the friends of the clergyman and his wife with his arguments, religious notions, his politics and his singular language. It will thus be guessed that he was a frequent visitor at Wyloe. But one day Fortescue received a letter from the owners of the Verulam saying that poor old William Stone had a week previously made his last stretch off shore and gone to rest in a graveyard in the neighbourhood of his well-beloved dock haunts.

Six months after the return of Fortescue and Agatha, there was placed in a conspicuous part of the church at Wyloe, a memorial tablet, on which was inscribed :—

SACRED TO THE MEMORY OF

MALCOLM HOPE,

An infant,

Who died at sea, on board the schooner

"Golden Hope,"

On the 14th August, 18—.

" He took a child and set him in the midst of them."

One summer day Malcolm Fortescue and his wife Agatha entered the church hand in hand.   They stood for a few minutes before this tablet, Agatha with her eyes fixed upon it, Fortescue watching her.

"Oh, Malcolm," she exclaimed, in a low, thrilling voice, with a look on her face of exquisite tenderness, " I remember!   Yes, it has all come back to me—poor little nameless one!"

Her eyes filled with tears, and thus weeping she knelt, her husband by her side, still hand in hand.

THE END.

TILLOTSON AND SON, PRINTERS, BOLTON.